DONOVAN

DONOVAN

DONOVAN

by

Max von Kreisler

The Golden West Large Print Books
Long Preston, North Yorkshire,
BD23 4ND, England.

British Library Cataloguing in Publication Data.

von Kreisler, Max
Donovan.

A catalogue record of this book is
available from the British Library.

ISBN 978-1-84262-954-3 pbk

Cover illustration © Michael Thomas

The moral right of the author has been asserted

Published in Large Print 2014 by arrangement with
Golden West Literary Agency

The Golden West Large Print is an imprint of Library Magna
Books Ltd.

Printed and bound in Great Britain by
T.J. (International) Ltd., Cornwall, PL28 8RW

Man and horse were both stumbling from exhaustion when they crested the Mogollon Rim. Loosening the cinch, the man poured the last of the water from his canteen and rinsed out the bay's dust-coated nostrils. Only then did he let it drink.

When the horse had finished, the man stretched out on his back and stared up at the pale blue sky. Although it was only September a strong, chill wind blew steadily from the north, soughing through the Ponderosa pines.

In the lee of the granite outcrop, away from the wind, the man relaxed, weariness bearing heavily down upon him. Save for brief periods of rest such as this, he had been in the saddle for the past seventy-two hours.

He had been on the run for three weeks.

Now he had reached the limits of his endurance. He had to find a place – and quickly – to make a stand.

He had at most three hours.

Gradually the sun warmed his chilled body. His eyelids dropped, snapped open.

Sleep and you're dead.

After half an hour, he rose and walked over to where the bay stood, spraddle-legged, nibbling dispiritedly on sparse bunch grass.

Like the man himself, his gear had seen better days. Yet, for all that, it had been well cared for. The carbine in the saddle boot had been recently cleaned and oiled, as had the .45 at his hip. The field glasses he fished out of his saddle bags were of top quality.

Other than these essentials, however, the grim, unrelenting chase had taken its toll of both man and horse.

The horse was finished.

So also, said half of Arizona Territory, was the man. A possibility which he accepted with the philosophical detachment of his kind. In his profession every hunt entailed a calculated risk.

He had been well aware of the danger of trying to bring in the Apache, Chaco, alive. Nor had he ignored the consequences of failure. But with five thousand dollars and a principle at stake he had gambled and lost.

Chaco had chosen to die a chief rather than at the end of a rope.

By his act he had also doomed his hunter.

Within hours, Chaco's friend, Delcha, and a score of braves had sworn vengeance.

8

For twenty days, faces black and ocher daubed, they had clung to the white man's trail, running their shaggy little ponies to death and then racing doggedly on foot until they could steal fresh horses.

Donovan had tried every trick he knew to shake them, but without success. At night the winking eyes of their camp fires mocked him from the darkness. At dawn and sunset they showed themselves arrogantly against the skyline, taunting him with soundless threats.

But if they hoped to break his courage, they had failed. Donovan and death had ridden too many trails together for the man to fear the shadow. Even when he realized that they were inexorably herding him away from small settlements like Sunflower, Rye, Jake's Corner, and Gisela, driving him steadily northward, he did not panic. He had plenty of ammunition, and as long as he could trade horses and pick up grub at remote ranch homes, he could hold his own. Eventually, Delcha and his bucks would cool off and abandon the chase.

He had misjudged them.

They had not given up. He realized now that they would never give up.

Although the knowledge disturbed him,

9

he had accepted it with typical objectivity. He would simply have to kill them off one at a time.

Within the first eight days he brought down three of them at long range. In return, he received a nasty flesh wound that was slow in healing.

After that, they had grown more cautious. And more clever.

Just how clever he did not realize until he rode into a ranch yard one day and found himself staring down the barrel of a Winchester held by a grim-faced cattleman.

'You the bounty hunter who killed that 'Pache, Chaco?'

'I'm Donovan.'

'Well, then, git!'

'Just a minute, friend,' Donovan said. 'I need food and a fresh horse. You can figure the difference.'

'To hell with your money! Delcha's spread the word that any man who lifts a hand to help you is good as dead. Now you just git 'fore he trails you here an' kills us all!' He glared at Donovan and his eyes reflected the bitterness of his voice.

'No trouble with 'Paches for years. Now you've gone an' stirred 'em up. Mister, you better stay clear of towns an' big ranches.

10

'Cause sooner or later someone's goin' to kill you. Or turn you over to Delcha. Now move on 'fore I git ideas myself.'

Donovan's lips thinned. 'You know what Chaco did to Senator Fleming's daughter?'

The rancher flushed. 'What's done is done. Gettin' a hundred more innocent people killed ain't goin' to change that.' He motioned with the rifle. 'Ride!'

After that, Donovan stole horses and stampeded the rest of the remuda to slow down pursuit, white and red alike. Food was a constant problem. He did not dare butcher a beef; buzzards would have betrayed his position. Nor did he dare shoot small game; the sound would have given him away. He lived, for the most part, off what he managed to steal from isolated ranches.

By this time half of Arizona Territory, south to Tucson, north to Flagstaff, and east to Globe and Holbrook, knew of the white man's plight.

Yet no one would lift a hand to help him.

Like a stallion being run down by wolves, he cut a desperate zigzag pattern across the high, lonely land with no real hope of escape.

By the time he reached the Mogollon Rim, he had come to accept the inevitability of death. But not to yield passively to it.

He meant to fight.

Turning now from the winded horse, he stretched out full length on the rocky point and swung the binoculars toward the pine studded sweep of land below. For five minutes he lay thus, unmoving save for the slow, careful arc of the field glasses. No signs of movement. Only the silent, lonely land with its...

The glasses stopped, steadied on a small, golden-tan valley a thousand feet below and a mile to the south.

Donovan adjusted the binoculars.

A cabin and several outbuildings came into focus.

A pale gray spiral of smoke curled upward.

Donovan rose, stuffed the glasses back into the bag. Then leading the wind-broken horse, he began to work his way slowly down the massive escarpment toward the pluming smoke.

Here in the valley, away from the chill wind sweeping the Mogollon Rim, the land drowsed quietly under a warm, Indian summer afternoon. In the half mile long meadow between the heavy timber and Christopher Creek, a score of sleek thoroughbreds grazed on the still plentiful grass.

To the south, where the meadow curved in a sickle shaped arc, a cabin of peeled logs and stone commanded approaches from north, east, and west, with the creek a natural barrier behind. A snug barn, corral, woodshed and smithy formed a compact group of outbuildings.

West of the cabin an orchard heavy with apples, peaches, winter pears, cherries and plums. Bordering the orchard, a vineyard of grapes, blackberries, loganberries, red raspberries and a bed of ever-bearing strawberries. A quarter acre vegetable garden still yielded corn, squash, tomatoes, cucumbers, onions, potatoes and green beans in abundance.

A sow grunted in the sty. There was a milch cow in the barn. And chickens scratched industriously in the yard for worms.

Peggy Simpson came out of the barn and walked toward the house, the milk in the tin bucket sloshing gently to the natural rhythm of her hips. A bobcat leaped from the woodshed, flashed in front of her and disappeared into the timber. She did not even see it. Her mind was two hundred miles away and four years in the past.

Halfway to the cabin, the screech of rusty metal shattered her dream memory and set her teeth on edge. She looked toward the windmill, a quick frown forming between her fine blue eyes at sight of the man working there.

She dreamed too much and she knew it; yet she resented being snapped back to reality so suddenly, especially by him. Of late, however, she was finding it more and more difficult to escape into the past and less satisfying when she did so. Perhaps because she was discovering the present to be far more rewarding, if not so thrilling.

Despite herself, her heart quickened. It was ridiculous, of course, to think that after being married to a man for almost four years she should begin to see him in a different light. Should even experience intimate emotions for him.

She had thought it could never happen to her again. And certainly not with quiet, mild-mannered Pete Simpson who seldom spoke to her, and when he did only about thoroughbred horses or the orchard or a fawn whose mother had been killed by a cougar.

Yet it was happening. Slowly, true, but happening just the same. Deepening, growing stronger as time passed.

Watching him now, struggling with a rusty gear, she realized that even her quick irritation was a defensive shield against him, against herself. He had become a threat to her past, and she did not want to surrender that.

She hesitated, then turned aside and walked the hundred feet to the windmill.

Pete Simpson straightened, wiped the perspiration from his face and smiled.

'Needed a bit of grease was all.' His voice was slow, careful. 'I don't think it'll bother you anymore.'

Color tinged her cheeks. She had complained that when the wind came up in the night the screech of the windmill awoke her and she couldn't go back to sleep.

Not even a day had passed and he'd already fixed it.

Had it been Monty ... why not admit it? Monty would have told her to plug her ears and stop bitching.

Even so, her 'Thank you, Pete,' was still almost formal, as though she were speaking to a hired man rather than her husband. Ashamed, she took the dipper from the water bucket beside the windmill and handed him a full measure of the still warm milk.

'Here!' Sharply. 'You'd better drink this. It's a good couple of hours until supper time.'

He drank slowly, tilting his head until the dipper was empty. He handed it back to her with an odd expression – as though he had received an unexpected kindness. He started to speak, swallowed, and then just stood there looking at her.

Caught by the moment, she searched his face for some sign of the change within him which was causing her all this emotional upheaval.

It was a face she had looked at a thousand times. Across the table, at work, on the pillow beside her at night. She knew its every line, every feature. Wind-tanned, a little too thin, the cheeks a trifle hollow. Pale blond hair, high forehead, calm, blue-gray eyes. The nose bent a little to the left from having been broken when he was a kid. The wide, mobile mouth, like the eyes, calm, patient.

Weak, easygoing, she thought, but was not so certain of this as she had been. Irritated, she turned abruptly and walked away, leaving him to stare after her with a dull hurt.

After a moment, he picked up his tools and headed for the barn. He put away the tools, wiped his hands, and with his favorite fishing rod headed for the creek.

He was standing knee deep in the swift rushing water, fishing, when Donovan came out of the timber behind him, leading the bay and limping on blistered feet.

For several minutes, Donovan remained motionless, watching the man in the creek. Then moving quietly to the bank, he said, 'You should never put your back to timber.'

The man started, tried to turn quickly in the rushing water, half fell and lost his fishing pole. Sloshing ashore, he wrung the water from his pants, pulled on his boots, and took in Donovan's six feet four, two hundred and thirty pound figure in a single glance. Then he retorted mildly:

'And you ought not to come up on a man that way.'

'If I'd been an Apache you'd be dead,' Donovan said. 'Don't you know better than to leave your house without a gun?'

The blond-haired man flushed. ''Paches haven't raided in the Rim country since I've been here. A good eight years.'

'They're raiding now,' Donovan retorted. 'All over the Territory, New Mexico and down into Sonora. Nachez, Geronimo, Victorio, *Del-she,* every anti-reservation chief.'

He turned to the bay, loosened the cinch and let the animal drink. When it had finished, Donovan unsaddled it and slapped it smartly on the rump. The bay trotted off, caught sight of the horses at the far end of the valley and broke into a weary gallop.

Noting the rancher's quick frown, Donovan said matter of factly:

'Delcha's hot on my trail. You can load your family in a buckboard and make a run for it. You might make it and you might not. I'd stay here. But that's up to you.'

Simpson paled. He threw a worried glance toward the cabin. When he turned back his face was set.

'I'm thirty-six years old,' he said. 'Too old to start over again. I'll stay.'

'What about your family? Any children?'

'A fourteen-year-old stepson.'

'He's big enough to handle a rifle.'

'He'd like nothing better,' Simpson replied bitterly. 'But I can't risk it. I'll send him and Peggy over to Pleasant Valley. There's a couple of good-sized ranches over there. If they can they'll send help. If not we'll just have to do the best we can. That is, unless...' His eyes met Donovan's.

'Those horses out there are thoroughbred racers. I breed and sell them to the stage lines. They can outrun any Indian pony living. You can take your pick.' He hesitated the barest fraction of a second.

'If you rode east and then circled to the south–'

'They'd never know about this place, would they?' Donovan said without rancour.

'No.'

'And you could go right on living like nothing had ever happened.'

'I'd remember that you made it possible.'

Although his voice was calm, Donovan sensed the man's quiet desperation. He would ask for the sake of his family; and for the long, hard years that had gone into the making of this place which was as much a part of him as his heart or his mind.

He would ask, but he would not beg.

There was a difference.

That was what decided Donovan.

He stood there in the warm afternoon sun, the rush of water over smooth, rounded stones lulling his tired mind, pulling his granulated eyelids down over his aching eyes, feeling the bone-aching weariness that permeated his whole body, the hunger pangs tormenting his stomach.

He thought of the bed inside the cabin, of the hot food that would soon be on the table, of the companionship, the sound of a woman's voice...

He thought of these things because he was

19

Donovan, and because, regardless of what the Territory believed, he was a human being.

And then he considered what might happen if he drew Delcha to this place. Someone would be killed. If it were he and the man, and the boy and the woman were left defenceless... He remembered what had happened to Senator Fleming's daughter.

That was a mistake, remembering.

He sighed, opened his burning eyes and nodded.

'Give me the fastest one of the bunch. And have your wife fix me a bag of food. If I shake them I'll send the horse back to you.'

'I ... I...' Simpson turned and strode rapidly toward the house.

Five minutes later, he returned carrying a rifle. Saddling the lone horse in the corral, he rode out to the herd.

He was trying to dap a loop over an elusive gray racer when Peggy Simpson came out of the cabin, shaded her eyes against the sun and walked swiftly toward Donovan.

The bounty hunter lay stretched out on his back beside the rushing creek, his head pillowed on his saddle. Sunlight filtered through the full-leafed oak, dappling his face.

Fascinated, Peggy Simpson stood for a moment, studying the sleeping stranger. She had never seen such a big man in her life. Not merely big but lean, like a smooth muscled cougar.

Yet it was not his size that held her but his face. Even in sleep, she had the distinct impression that the eyes behind the lowered lids were watching her. That the mind behind the impassive features never really slept, but only withdrew into itself for short periods of rest.

It was an odd feeling and she reacted to it with mixed emotions. Hostility, fear, curiosity, fascination, and an almost embarrassing sense of intimacy.

She had never seen him before, never spoken to him; she did not even know his name. Yet she sensed that if he should suddenly open his eyes and look at her, he would know her for what she was, what she had been, and what she was becoming.

She would have no secrets from him, no defenses; and, unless he left immediately, no escape.

Despite the warm afternoon sun, she shivered. Without ever having seen the color of his eyes or having heard the sound of his voice, she was suddenly afraid of him.

Leaving the sack of food, she hurried back

to the house.

She had just reached the porch when the crack of the rifle whiplashed the length of the valley. She whirled and saw Pete quirting the herd toward the corral and behind him dark skinned riders pressing close, and then she screamed, 'Oh, my God! *Tommy!*' and raced for the barn.

She took a dozen running steps and then Donovan's rifle went off and somewhere out there in the meadow a man screamed in agony. She kept running, and the rifle kept cracking, and now she could hear the shrill yipping cries, like a bunch of coyotes in full chorus.

Tommy came bursting out of the barn, a pitch fork in his hand, his face dark, sullen, intense.

'What's all the commotion about, Ma?'

'Get in the house!' She grabbed his arm and gave him a violent shove. 'Shoot anything that's not white!'

Ignoring his protests, she raised her skirts and ran for the corral. If the herd hit the gate half of them would be maimed or killed.

The gate was already open. The stranger had already foreseen the problem.

As she started to turn back toward the house, she became aware of the earth vibrating under her feet. Too late, she heard the thrumming of hoofs. Over her shoulder she caught a kaleidoscopic glimpse of flying manes, wall eyes, and flaring nostrils. And of Pete, staring straight at her, trapped in the middle of the herd, with horrified eyes.

I'm going to die, she thought. *I'm going to be trampled into a bloody...*

A huge pair of shoulders blocked out the nightmare and a pistol started banging in her ear and the stranger was shouting and waving his hat at the onrushing horses and, at the last instant, the herd parted and swept past, churning up a choking cloud of dust as it milled around in the corral.

Somehow, she managed to turn before her legs gave way. Only a strong arm around her waist kept her from falling.

'Are you all right?'

She had thought his voice would be harsh, filled with violence, and was surprised by its calm, impersonal quality. Reluctantly, she raised her eyes to him then immediately retreated behind lowered lids. She began to shiver, conscious of his arm around her, of his almost overpowering maleness.

'Are you all right?' he repeated.

Not looking at him, she nodded. 'I think so. If ... if...' She swallowed, made a frantic little gesture with her hand and fled to the house leaving Donovan with a vivid impression of long black hair, startling blue eyes and a firm, pliant body.

He was still standing there, frowning slightly, when Pete Simpson rushed up. The rancher's face was pale.

'My God! Is she all right?'

'I think she lost her dinner.'

Simpson walked over to the corral. He studied the milling horses for a moment, then said quietly, 'How do I thank you?'

'For what?' Donovan said. 'I was thinking of myself.'

Simpson swung around. 'With the 'Paches, yes. And maybe with the horses. You needed a racer. But Peggy...' He shook his head. 'You almost got yourself killed. I'll be indebted to you the rest of my life.'

'It may be a short indebtedness.' Donovan jerked a thumb to the east. 'They were closer than I thought.'

His eyes ranged over the thoroughbreds in the corral. *Beauty, speed, stamina.* God, what he wouldn't have given for one of them three weeks ago! That steel gray, for instance. With a horse like that under him he could have outrun Delcha to Tucson.

Right now, he would be sitting relaxed in

Carmelia Ortega's house, watching the light play across her face as the fiery rhythms of young Victorio's guitar quickened his pulse.

He had promised Victorio that he would send him to Spain to study under Faella. He had promised him many things. He would live to keep none of them. Here under the Mogollon Rim he would die and Victorio, not knowing, would wonder why it was that his one friend had betrayed him.

Grimly he thrust the thought aside to destroy the last hope which still lingered in the rancher's mind.

'You might as well forget it,' he said. 'They'd bring me down before I got a hundred yards.'

'Even on a racer?'

'Even if the racer had wings.' Donovan fed fresh shells into the Winchester and swung it in a full circle. 'They've got us surrounded.'

'One of us might slip through after dark for help.'

'Not a chance.'

Simpson breathed deeply. 'How many are there?'

'Twelve or fifteen, not counting their dead.'

'What are our chances?'

Donovan hauled out the makings, rolled a cigarette, lit it and stared thoughtfully out across the valley.

'You've lived in this country for eight years and you ask me that?'

Simpson flushed. 'I've never fought 'Paches.'

'All right.' Donovan dragged on his cigarette and then ground it out under his heel. 'I'll tell you. With luck, a fifty-fifty chance. If one of us is killed: no chance at all.'

'You paint a bleak picture.'

'You wanted the truth,' Donovan reminded him. Then: 'What about supplies?'

The rancher shrugged. 'We don't go into Green Valley very often so we stay pretty well stocked on staples. Enough for a couple of months, not counting the garden and the fruit.'

'Water?'

'The windmill pumps it to the house and I've channeled creek water to the corral.'

'What about guns and ammunition?'

'Two Winchesters, a forty-four, and a Greener. A hundred rounds for the rifles, fifty for the pistol, and a couple of boxes of shells for the shotgun.'

Donovan whistled softly. With the cabin commanding approaches from three sides and the creek slowing down any attack from the timber, their position was all but impregnable. A frontal assault across five hundred yards of open meadow would be suicide. And well equipped with food, water and ammunition, a long drawn-out siege would be impractical.

Yet it was a siege that Donovan feared. For although he did not know the man beside him, he knew human nature and the courses it could take. The outcome of the present situation was already predictable.

Two men, a woman, and a fourteen-year-old boy cooped up in a cabin day after day, constantly scanning the empty valley for some sign of movement. Listening, sleepless, to the night sounds, reading in each one an imminent threat. Waiting, nerves screaming, for the swift rush of moccasined feet. Gradually, as the days passed and the tension mounted, growing more critical of one another until dislike took on the dark undertones of hate and the masks began to slip and their true natures emerged.

Then these people would remember who was responsible for their predicament. Who had brought the Apaches down upon them to begin with. And gradually, because they *were* civilized, they would admit to themselves how easy it would be to get rid of the Apaches.

Get rid of the man who had brought them here.

It was bound to happen, Donovan realized. When it did he would deal with it. Meanwhile, he would do what he could to consolidate his defenses.

Turning back to Simpson, he said, 'You'd better check your guns and break out your ammunition. And have your wife cook us something. When it's ready, call me. I'll keep a look-out from the barn.'

'Wait.' The rancher regarded him steadily. 'Who are you anyway? And why are those 'Paches after your hide?'

Deliberately Donovan let the moment drag out. When he answered his voice was cold.

'My name's Donovan. I'm a bounty hunter. Five months ago Chaco, a friend of Delcha's, attacked a stagecoach carrying Senator Fleming's nineteen-year-old daughter. The girl was the sole survivor. Chaco took her captive. When she became pregnant he sold her to a *comanchero* who ransomed her to Senator Fleming for five thousand dollars. A week later the girl killed herself.

'The Senator offered a two thousand dollar reward for Chaco, dead or alive. I tried to bring him in for trial. He was a brave man. I had to kill him.' Donovan's eyes flickered once more to the thoroughbreds in the corral.

'Before I could reach Tucson Delcha and his bucks cut me off. I couldn't shake them. They've chased me all over the Territory. They won't give up until I'm dead.'

'And us along with you.' Simpson couldn't keep the bitterness from his voice.

As Donovan moved toward the barn, the rancher called after him. 'What'll I tell my wife?'

'Tell her the truth,' Donovan said. 'Not to get caught with an empty gun.'

Simpson shivered, then hurried toward the house.

In the hay mow, Donovan settled down before the window. Overlooking the creek, it offered a clear view of the sweeping arc of timber. It would be from there that the attack would come.

The shadows lengthened, reaching out toward the corral. Beyond the orchard, the Mazatals dimmed to a misty gray.

In the corral, a fly-tormented horse rolled in the dust. The rest of the herd stood, hip-shot, drowsing in the still warm afternoon sun.

Atop a pinon tree, a jay-bird balanced against a freshening breeze.

Donovan knelt, motionless, to one side of the mow window watching the horses, the jay-bird, and the edge of the timber. Gradually, the silence, the lengthening shadows, and lack of sleep pulled his granulated eyelids down. His head bowed. The warm quiet of the mow began to slip away.

Suddenly, a horse whickered and the jay-bird set up a raucous din.

Donovan's eyes snapped open. The Winchester whipped up in a single motion.

Facing the timber, the horses shifted restlessly, ears perked, nostrils flaring.

Donovan jacked a shell into the Winchester and waited.

The minutes dragged on.

The herd started to move around.

Suddenly, the jay-bird took off, screeching.

They came out of the timber, bent low, running without sound.

Donovan opened fire.

An Apache spun and fell halfway to the creek. Another stained the water with his blood. A snap shot at Delcha missed.

Gunfire crackled from the cabin and another man went down.

Caught in a cross fire, the Apaches faded

back into the timber, taking their dead with them.

For half an hour, Donovan knelt with the Winchester at the ready. Finally, when the horses drifted away from the creek side of the corral and the jay-bird returned to the pinon, he relaxed and watched the sky shade from brilliant red to pink to purple and imperceptibly blend into gray.

'Donovan!' Simpson shouted from the cabin. 'Are you all right?'

'Yes.'

'I'm coming out.'

'Stay where you are!'

Fifteen minutes. Half an hour.

The light flowing through the mow dimmed, disappeared, and then the window became a black square of velvet strewn with diamonds as the stars blazed through the thin, dry atmosphere.

Donovan stood up and stretched. Then he climbed down the ladder and stepped outside.

He stood motionless, breathing deeply of the already chill air. Tilting his head he looked up at the stars, incredibly brilliant at this altitude, and wondered why it was that man had never found the answer to them.

In the corral, the horses, dark bulks in the star sheen, moved about quietly now. Later, he decided, he would stable as many of them as possible in the barn.

Twenty feet from the cabin, he stopped and whistled softly.

'Simpson!'

'Yes?'

'I'm coming in.'

He entered quickly and closed the door.

'Light a lamp!'

Flame flickered from the stove's open firebox. Someone lit a lamp with a pine splinter.

'Cover the windows!' Donovan snapped, then saw that they were already covered.

'Is it over?' Simpson asked.

'For the time being.'

Donovan turned his attention to the woman. The memory of her had been with him during those hours in the warm, silent mow. The feel of her firm body, the swell of her breasts against his encircling arm, the full, parted lips...

It had been a month since he had had a woman. Not long perhaps to some men, but Donovan's big body demanded frequent releases from the fierce, secret drives which he kept carefully hidden from others.

He studied her now, her figure caught in

the yellow glow of the lamp light, her hair, blue-black as a Castilian's, falling down over her shoulders. Taller than he had thought, five feet eight or nine. Sensuous. The brilliant blue eyes, the wide, full-lipped mouth, everything about her ... even the slight shrug of her shoulders as she turned away from his bold glance ... was sensuous.

She was the most beautiful woman Donovan had ever seen. She was more than that. It showed in her eyes, in the ripe mouth, sullen with dissatisfaction.

As she turned toward the kitchen range, the startling blue eyes met his and he saw quick fear flood them.

He knew why.

He wondered if she did.

Wearily, he sat down at the kitchen table.

She brought him coffee, black and steaming, and he drank it while Simpson and the boy slipped outside and the woman busied herself at the stove, not looking at him.

She served him food, refilled his coffee cup and moved back to the stove, her hips swinging with a totally unconscious grace. Putting the coffee pot on the stove, she came back and stood beside him.

'I want to thank you for what you did,' she said. 'I've never been that close to death before. If it hadn't been for you...' She shrugged and even that simple gesture carried an expressive grace.

Donovan lit a cigarette and regarded her without false pretense.

'If it hadn't been for me your troubles would all be over.'

'I've never been one to run from trouble, Mister Donovan.'

'No,' he said. 'That's been your weakness.'

Her face shadowed, but she did not drop her gaze. 'You pride yourself in knowing women, don't you?'

'Some women.'

'Like me?'

He finished his coffee, put the cup down, and said, 'Why are you afraid of me?'

'Am I?' Her voice was challenging. 'I wasn't aware of it.'

'You've been afraid of me from the first moment you saw me. Why?'

In the lamp light, her face took on a bitter, disillusioned cast. 'Why ask when you obviously know?'

Donovan shrugged. 'A man can never be sure of anything. Especially a woman.'

She flushed. 'Owing you my life, Mr Donovan, doesn't mean I have to like you.'

Nothing could have brought Donovan up

so sharply. She had thanked him for saving her life and he had taken advantage of her gratitude. He had no right to pry into her personal nature. Nor to desire her.

He had no right, but he did.

'You owe me nothing, Mrs...?'

'I'm Peggy Simpson,' she said. 'And I think you should know that Pete ... well, that my husband knows all about me.'

'Does he?' Donovan rose, picked up his hat and went outside.

A shadow detached itself from the big oak near the cabin.

Donovan's rifle came up. 'Simpson?'

'Yes. Did you eat?'

'Uh-huh.' Donovan joined the rancher. 'Where is the boy?'

Simpson pointed to a tree some thirty feet away.

'Call him over.'

'Tommy!'

'Yeah?'

'Mister Donovan wants to talk to you.'

The boy slipped across the clearing. 'Yeah? What do you want?'

Donovan looked him over. Already, at fourteen, Tommy Lord was taller than his stepfather. But there was none of Pete Simpson's character in the boy's features.

Studying the handsome face with its sneering mouth, insolent mouth and smugly superior expression, Donovan frowned. The boy reminded him of someone he had known somewhere, sometime. Impatiently, he brushed the thought aside. He had seen a thousand Tommy Lords in his life. Not one of them had been worth a damn.

Young Lord shifted uncomfortably under the big man's hard eyes. 'Yeah? What do you want?'

'When a man talks to you, boy,' Donovan said, 'you say *Mister*. Do you understand?'

'You really think you're something, don't you?' the kid sneered. 'Well, just because you're big as a barn an' killed a few 'Paches don't mean...'

For a man his size Donovan moved with amazing speed. He grabbed the boy, draped him across his knee, and while Pete Simpson looked on, laid a heavy hand against the boy's rear. Then setting him down, he said coldly:

'Another thing, boy. Never talk back to a man until you're able to fight him.'

'You big bastard!' the kid cried. 'Someday I'll kill you for that!' Whirling on his stepfather, he yelled, 'Why'd you stand there an' let him beat me? You scared of him? Sure you

36

are! No wonder Ma's got no respect for you.'

'You had it coming to you,' Simpson retorted. 'Now go ahead. Run to your mother. That's what you usually do.'

'You're not going anywhere, boy,' Donovan said. 'Your mother's got troubles enough without your snivelling.'

'I hate you!' Tommy Lord's face contorted with passion. 'I hate you both! Someday...'

'Shut up!' The menace in Donovan's voice silenced the boy like a gag. *'And listen!'*

'What do you think?' Simpson switched the subject. 'Will they attack again tonight?'

Donovan shook his head. 'No, they'll wait until just before dawn. But they may try and steal the horses. So we'll keep three hour watches. At four-thirty everybody will be up. You'd better join me in the barn then. They'll come at us out of the timber.'

'What about Tommy?' Simpson sounded skeptical. 'He's only fourteen, Donovan.'

'He's good at shooting off his mouth,' Donovan retorted. 'Let's see how good he is with a gun.'

'Don't you worry about me,' the boy cried. 'I'll knock off my share of them 'Paches.'

Donovan's smile was grim. 'You'd better if you want to stay alive.' He nodded to Simpson.

'I'll take the first watch. Relieve me in three hours. Tommy'll you'll stand your turn later.'

He strode toward the barn, massive, uncompromising, the rifle swinging easily in his hand.

Already he had forgotten them.

Peggy Simpson served her husband in silence, her mind preoccupied with the man Donovan. She was thoroughly frightened, not so much of the man as the situation. Although she pretended not to understand the nature of that situation, she wasn't really fooling herself. She understood it only too well.

Yet not even Monty had ever suspected the truth. Monty had thought he knew women. He hadn't. If he had known her, he would have killed her. He was that much of an egoist. But since it had pleased him to believe that the things which she had done had been for the love of him, it had not been hard to conceal the truth. From him, but not from herself.

She knew.

Even while she was doing it, even while her body was arching upward in frenzied passion, it made her sick. Like a second helping of food when one was already full. The hunger was all in her mind. And no amount of passion could ever satisfy it.

She looked at Pete seated across from her, his eyes on his plate because to look at her would mean to speak and he never knew what to say.

For some reason, during the past few months it had become increasingly important that Pete never found out the truth. Living out here, isolated from people, had helped. Until today she had actually thought she had conquered it. Now she knew better.

So did the man Donovan. The knowledge that he could torture her, play with her emotions in secret amusement and, if he chose, destroy her, was all but intolerable.

Abruptly, she rose and crossed to the blanketed window. The old restlessness filled her, the sense of inadequacy, the desperate need for reassurance, for completeness. She lifted a corner of the blanket and stared out across the almost bright-as-day clearing.

She thought of Donovan, massive, virile, out there in the barn, and felt the heat rise in her.

Damn you, Donovan, get out of my life! Ride out of here now before you destroy me. Before you destroy us all!

Pete Simpson finished his meal, drained his coffee cup and sat staring morosely at his wife at the window. Strange how a man could live with a woman, work with her, sleep with her month after month, year after year, and never really know her.

Part of it was his fault, maybe all of it. He had never been able to talk to people. It was like being shut up in a room, able to look out and see people, but unable to make himself heard no matter how hard he tried.

It all went back to his childhood.

Children should be seen, not heard. What a silly question! You mean you don't know? Shut up, boy, when grown-ups are talking! How far are the stars? What difference does it make? You better start learning to put in a crop, boy, instead of talking nonsense. Stars!

Frequently administered reprimands – willow switch, leather strap, and, as he grew older, a heavy hand taught young Pete a lesson. *Keep your mouth shut and you won't get hurt.*

That philosophy, for that was what it eventually became, he took with him when he left the farm on the Missouri and hit out on his own.

He had not hated his father. They had

simply not understood one another. Mainly because Hurd Simpson had never learned to listen to anyone.

Of his mother, Pete remembered only that she, too, had learned the value of silence. Save on those occasions when she had stood between him and his father. Even then she did not talk. She just stood looking at his father with a serene expression on her face until the miracle happened. And it always did.

Slowly, the red would fade from Hurd's cheeks. His breathing would ease. He would shift uneasily from one foot to the other. His eyes would slide away from Amy Simpson's. And then he would say gruffly, 'All right. Forget it. It's not that important.'

But to him, it *had* been important. What had been more important, however, was that Hurd Simpson had loved his wife and she had known it. She had known it because he had constantly proven it.

Hurd Simpson felt that words were pretty empty things. It was what a man did that counted, not what he said. And if he used a heavy hand to try and teach that to his sons – he had had five, including Pete – he could not be greatly faulted. At least that was the way Pete still looked at it, even after all these years. A man had to live the way he believed, no matter how harsh it might seem to others.

As he grew older, Pete Simpson realized why his father had been so strict. At one time, Hurd Simpson's mouth had gotten him into serious trouble. He was determined that the same thing should not happen to his sons for the very simple reason that he loved them.

And so Pete Simpson worked hard, kept his mouth shut, stayed out of trouble and saw a lot of country.

Barely sixteen when civil war split the nation and men marched off to die for whatever it was they believed in – he was too young to understand anything except that no man ought to be treated like an animal just because his skin was black.

Cannon thunder, crack of rifles, blood, screams, agony and hate. And then it was all over except the hate; and because he kept his mouth shut even that passed him by.

'68. Up the trail from Texas to Abilene with a herd of wild, lean longhorns, wrangling green-broke broncs for twenty-five dollars a month and found. For the first time in his life finding something he liked. *Horses*. But not the bottom of the barrel status of a horse wrangler with a cow outfit.

Next, a stint with *Wells-Fargo* tooling a fast stage across Arizona Territory. Hard, grueling, dangerous work, but it paid a hundred dollars a month and clothing at cost. Lonely up there on the box with the shotgun but he didn't mind. He loved the wild, sweeping land, especially the vast, aching immensity of the Mogollons. High, rugged country that brought him close to the stars Hurd Simpson had mocked.

He saved his money and in '73 he came to the valley, built the cabin, bought a half dozen brood mares and a blooded stallion and turned horse rancher.

Even after the coming of the railroad, he had a ready market for his racers with a dozen feeder lines operating in Colorado, New Mexico and Arizona Territory as well as in California.

His reputation spread. Soon individual buyers from all over the west, people who loved fine horses, came to buy from him. He sold to a few hard-faced men who rode in on jaded horses, paid in gold, and left even faster than they had come.

By the time he met and married Peggy Lord, under somewhat unusual circumstances, he could look to the future with optimism. If the marriage had not turned out quite the way he had hoped, he did not regret it. He still cherished dreams of a son and of a time when Peggy might feel differently toward him.

Meanwhile, he would wait.

He was still waiting when Donovan rode into his life with a bunch of Apaches hot on his trail, threatening by his very presence to destroy not only everything he had worked to build up, but everything he loved as well.

Tell her the truth. Not to get caught with an empty gun.

Donovan had meant it. Although they had beaten off two attacks, the odds were still six or seven to one. What would those odds be after daybreak tomorrow? Would they even be alive to care?

He knew that he should be sleeping. Soon he would have to relieve Donovan in the barn. But worry made sleep impossible. If anything happened to Peggy...

Damn you, Donovan, why didn't you straddle that gray and make a run for it? You might have made it. Anyway, you would have led them away from us. Why did you have to ride in here and turn our lives upside down? We don't owe you anything.

Only they did. They owed him their lives.

Turning away from the window, Peggy Simpson came back and sat down beside her husband. Her eyes were thoughtful, suspicious. The fear within her she kept well hidden.

'I've never seen a man like him,' she said. 'He's frozen fire that's never been thawed. Who is he? What is he?'

Simpson shifted uncomfortably. It was an issue he had hoped to avoid, knowing the violent reaction it would set off. But he sensed a restless tension in his wife that it would be unwise to antagonize. Once she got her mind set on something she was not easily side-tracked. He sighed and reconciled himself to the inevitable.

'He's a bounty hunter.'

She was too tired, too upset to grasp the meaning of what he had said. 'You mean he hunts for a living? Like cougars and wolves?'

'In a manner of speaking.'

'What do you mean?' Alert, suspicious now. 'In a manner of speaking?'

Simpson cleared his throat, then said reluctantly, 'Well, some of the men he hunts are animals, worse than a lot of animals.'

'*Men!*' Her voice shrilled with belated understanding. 'You mean he's a *man* hunter? A rotten killer who hunts down men for the reward money?'

'He doesn't look at it that way.'

She glared at him. 'And just how does he look at it?'

'Well, to him it's just another job. Like ranching or farming or mining. Somebody's got to do it. Sheriffs can't just drop everything and spend all their time looking for a single man. It's a specialized job.'

'God!' She stared at him, her mouth twisting with disgust. 'And you intend to let him stay? You'll fight that bunch of Apaches out there until they kill us all to try and save him? So that he can bring more innocent men back to die at the end of a rope like Monty!'

'Monty wasn't innocent, Peggy.' Pete Simpson's voice sharpened. 'He killed a man in cold blood. And it was a jury, not that bounty hunter, who sent him to the gallows. He got what was coming to him.'

'You've no right to say that!'

'I've every right to say it.'

'He was my husband! I loved him!'

'He's been dead going on four years, Peggy.'

Her eyes glistened with quick tears. 'He'll never be dead to me! When are you going to realize that?'

'Do you have to keep reminding me?'

'The truth's the truth! You knew I didn't love you when I married you.'

'Yes, but I had hoped that with time...' He shook his head, unable to express the emotions, the thoughts trapped inside him. During these moments, her hostility always filled him with an overpowering sense of futility.

'You had no right to hope,' she replied coldly. 'Before you called in the preacher I told you the truth so there would be no misunderstanding. A widow alone on the frontier, with a growing son to bring up, *has* to get married. It was a practical arrangement. Love had nothing to do with it. If you hadn't been willing, I'd have found someone else.'

'By God,' he cried, 'but you make it sound cold-blooded!'

'I don't believe in being hypocritical.'

'No one can accuse you of that!'

Peggy rose, refilled their coffee cup from the pot on the stove, and then sat down again. Resting her arms on the table, she gave him a cool, impersonal glance.

'You've no right to complain, Pete. I've kept your house, cooked your meals, mended your clothes, worked alongside you, and slept with you at night. What more do you want?'

'Is that all marriage means to you?' Simpson said. 'Keeping house, mending, cooking, sleeping?'

'I've had the other kind.'

'Well, I haven't!' He could not keep the resentment from his voice. 'Did you ever stop to think about that?'

She stirred sugar into her coffee, tested it, then set down her cup. 'Do you want me to leave if we live past this?'

'You know better than that. All I want is a son to carry on my name. Is that asking too much?'

'You've got Tommy.'

'Tommy is Monty's child, not mine.'

She hesitated, as though weighing his words. Then she shook her head. 'I'm old-fashioned, Pete. A child should be a love symbol.'

'My God, isn't my love enough for the both of us?'

Her mouth lost its fullness. 'A child would grow up to know the difference. No, Pete.'

'Tell me...' He brought his hand down sharply on the table. 'What in God's name did Monty Lord have that's missing in me?'

'He was a man's man.'

Had she spoken in anger, Simpson could

have rationalized away the remark and thus have saved his pride. But she did not grant him that merciful escape. Not that she meant to deliberately hurt him. That was not her nature. She simply had a shattering habit of saying exactly what she felt.

Had he not known this he might well have struck her in the swift upsurge of anger and humiliation that swept him.

It would have been kinder than what he did.

'Man's man, be damned!' he cried. 'Monty Lord was nothing but a high living, quick tempered, tin horn gambler who wasn't above selling his wife for the night to pay off his gambling debts!'

Peggy sat looking at him for a long time. When she finally spoke, her voice was as gray and lifeless as her face.

'That's been festering in your mind for a long time, hasn't it, Pete? Why don't you come out and say I was a whore?'

He remained silent, hating himself, knowing that he had destroyed his last hope of happiness. The thing was done, said. She would never forget or forgive. Yet he had not meant to hurt her. He had simply spoken a truth about Monty Lord and she had been cut by the backlash.

'What you were never made any difference to me,' he said dully. 'You know that. You've always been something special. Someone to love and cherish. And you have been a good wife. No man could ask for better.

'I guess if you were happy it wouldn't matter so much how you felt about me. But you're not happy. You keep on living with a phony memory. You won't face up to the fact that Monty Lord wasn't fit to sit in the same room with you.

'Sure, he was flashy. And he had a way with women. But smart people saw right through him. There wasn't a decent man in the Territory who would spit on him.'

'Or a decent woman?'

'You were in love,' Pete Simpson said gently. 'And no woman in love can think clearly.'

You still don't know the truth, do you, Pete?

His naiveness amazed her. His simplicity touched her, washed away her anger. She laid a hand on his arm in a rare gesture of intimacy.

'I'm not in love with you, Pete. You know that. Maybe it's because you're so quiet and easygoing. Almost as if you didn't have any guts or principles at all. But, lately, I'd begun to wonder if, in a different way, you weren't

50

more of a man than Monty ever was.

'Now *this* happens. You'll throw away everything we've worked to build up. You'll even sacrifice me, who you claim to love, to try and save a damn bounty hunter.' Anger took hold of her once more, making her forget the compassion she had felt for him only moments before.

'Do you understand, Pete?' she cried. *'For a damn bounty hunter!'*

Simpson ran a hand through his thinning hair with a harried gesture. 'What do you expect me to do?'

She leaned forward, bringing her face close to his, her eyes merciless.

'Put a gun in his back and tell him to make a run for it. Or turn him over to them. I don't care which. Just get rid of him!'

'I can't do that!'

'Why not? Tell me, why not?'

'Because he's a human being.'

'He's a beast!' she cried savagely. 'Worse than a beast because he hunts down his own kind!'

'We owe him our lives.'

'Only because he brought down a bunch of murdering Apaches on us to begin with!'

Pete Simpson put down his coffee cup with a slow deliberation. He had expected a reaction from her, but nothing as violent as this. It all went back of course, to Monty Lord and the bounty hunter who had brought him in. It was impossible for her to separate Donovan from that unknown man.

Still, he tried to reason with her.

'Donovan's done what any living creature will try to do. Save his own life. You can't blame him for that.'

'Would you act the same way in his place?'

'I'd have to be in his place before I could answer that.'

Her face paled. 'Then you won't send him away? Even if it means the death of all of us, including me?'

'No.'

'Monty would have.'

His smile was a painful twist of the lips. 'I'm not Monty, Peggy.'

'No, you're not Monty!' she flung at him. 'You're not much of anything!'

He sat silent, her words scalding his mind.

'Look at me, Pete!'

He raised his head.

She stood over him, her face suddenly smooth as porcelain.

'I want you to listen carefully.' All the anger was gone from her voice. 'I'm not going to die for scum like this man Donovan. The minute he turns his back I'll kill him myself. With gun, a knife, a hatchet, whatever I can lay my hands on.

'Then if we live through this I'm going to leave you, Pete. I'm going to find me a man with guts. One who knows the difference between right and wrong and isn't afraid to stand up and be counted. And I'm going to parade him back and forth in front of you until you can't take it anymore and end up blowing your brains out.

'Do you hear me, Pete?' Voice high, thin. *'Do you understand?'*

'I'll not send him away.'

'Goddamn you!'

She put her back to him then; and in that moment Pete Simpson realized that all their years together had meant nothing to her. She could and would erase them as though they had never been.

Wearily, he rose and went outside.

When he had gone, Peggy Simpson sat down at the table and buried her face in her hands. She cried for the first time since Monty's death. Hard, shuddering protests against the empty, futile years of her life. But most of all, against this man who had begun to stir her heart in a way that Monty Lord had never done.

Over near the oak tree, Tommy Lord heard the cabin door open and close and straightened, his hands gripping the Winchester tightly. He did not want to admit it but he was scared. The sight of those 'Paches breaking out of the timber and racing toward the creek had been terrifyingly real. Until then, it had been a game with him bragging how he would drop them like rabbits. But when it had actually happened he had panicked.

His cheeks burned, remembering Pete's quiet voice saying, 'Just squeeze off your shots easy-like.' And when the rifle butt had slammed against his shoulder: 'That's the idea, boy. A little lower and you'd have had him.'

Afterward, Pete had said, 'You think you were the only one scared? *Look!*' He'd held up a shaking hand but Tommy hadn't been fooled. When a man's hand shook that way his voice was bound to shake, too. But Pete Simpson's voice had been as calm as though he were saying, 'It's a nice day, huh, kid?'

That made it bad, his stepfather pretending just so's he, Tommy, could save face. He had no use for the mealy-mouthed fool and he wanted no favors from him.

He knew why his mother had married

Pete. A pure and simple case of having to. Either that or starve. She'd have rather starved if it hadn't been for him. But why'd she have to settle for Pete Simpson? There were plenty of real men she could have had. She was a pretty woman; and he'd seen the way men looked at her when she walked down the street.

One thing still puzzled him. Why did she have to marry at all? What had happened to the money his father had left her? He just couldn't believe that Monty Lord had died a pauper. Why, all those fine hats an' expensive broadcloth suits an' fancy vests an' spotless linen. An' the diamond studs an' the boots so shiny you could see your face in them. An' the fine restaurants an' the best hotels an'...

Of course ... his mind tried to shy away from the thought. Of course, there *had* been times when things hadn't been so good. Like leaving shabby hotels in the middle of the night, walking real quiet past the dozing desk clerk. Cheap cafes, greasy food and sometimes none at all. The fine suits threadbare, the linen frayed at the cuffs, the diamond studs missing, and the boots not quite so bright.

But heck, a man couldn't ride high an' wide all the time. There were bound to be days when the cards didn't fall right. All the same, his Dad had done pretty good until that stupid cowpoke had accused him of cheating. Monty had thought the fool was going for a gun and had shot him. He'd *had* to!

Why hadn't the jury believed that? Couldn't they see that Monty Lord was no blamed tin-horn, like the prosecutor claimed, who'd killed a couple of men in the past? Monty had not been like that, no matter what folks said. He'd been big time. Smart, polite, handsome and educated.

Dammit, why'd they have to stand him up on a scaffold an' put a rope around his neck an'...

Tears welled up in his eyes and he leaned against the tree until he had control of himself.

He was dry-eyed when Pete Simpson emerged from the darkness.

'See or hear anything?' Simpson asked.

'Nope.'

'You'd better get some sleep. We'll all have to be up before daybreak.'

The boy's jaw ridged. 'I'm not sleepy.'

'You will be,' Simpson said mildly, 'as soon as you hit the hay.'

When the boy did not answer, Simpson

propped his rifle against the tree and breathed deeply of the crisp air.

'You know that rifle of yours helped this afternoon, Tom. Come morning it'll count a lot more if you're wide awake. It could help save your mother's life.'

'Ma's your worry.' Deliberate, insolent. 'Dad always looked after her without no one's help.'

'Did he?' Simpson retorted. 'Then why did she have to...' He bit off the angry words. 'I'm not going to argue with you. Get in the house! You've been trying to act like a man for the past year. Now start being one! You may never have another chance!'

Without a word, the kid headed for the cabin.

One of these days he's stomp the son of a bitch into the ground! Maybe not right away. He'd have to grow a bit more first. But he'd do it. Hell, Monty would have whipped the tail off his horse wrangler!

But later, after he'd eaten and crawled into his bunk, he lay staring up into the darkness and grudgingly admitted that Pete had done a pretty good job of busting up that 'Pache charge across the creek.

Pete an' that fellow Donovan.

In the next room, Peggy Simpson, tensely awake, was thinking the same thing. Why hadn't Pete shown this strong side of himself before? She'd never forgive him for what he had said. Or for the decision he had made.

Well, it had been his decision, not hers. A man either loved her or he didn't. If he did then he should be willing to prove it.

Monty hadn't. But then he hadn't loved her either. She knew that; she'd known it for years. When was she going to stop kidding herself and admit it?

Her mind skidded away from the thought only to be trapped by an even more disturbing speculation.

When would Donovan be able to leave? And until he did, what was going to happen between them, cooped up this way?

The possibility was a frightening threat, an agonizing torment. Far more so than the Apaches out there in the night waiting to kill her.

Donovan, the hunter, and her, the prey.

Was it only in her mind? Did she really fear him? Or did she fear the hunger within her, the dark side of her own nature?

Was it Donovan, after all, who was the hunter? Or was it she who was the huntress?

In the mow, Donovan heard the barn door open and close and then the squeak of hinges. He called out, 'Simpson?'

'Yes. I'm coming up.'

Relaxing, Donovan laid aside the rifle as the rancher climbed into the mow.

Simpson's face was tense and a new sharpness edged his voice when he spoke.

'Sorry I'm late. I had a little trouble with the boy.'

'He needs his ass kicked,' Donovan said succinctly.

'He'll get it from now on,' Simpson said. 'I've had enough of his lip. *My Pa was this, my Pa was that!* His father was nothing but a flashy, two-bit gambler! It's time, by God, he faced up to the fact!'

It was the first show of anger Donovan had seen in the man. The iron beneath the mild-mannered surface was now beginning to show.

'You may have waited too long,' Donovan observed. 'But then that's your problem.'

'And one I'm fed up with.' Simpson moved over and took position beside the mow window. 'See anything?'

'No.'

'Maybe they've gone.'

Donovan stood up, stretching his big frame to ease his stiff muscles. 'They're still out there.'

'How do you know?'

'I can sense it.'

Settling himself so that he had a clear view of the creek and corral, Simpson checked his rifle with the same methodical thoroughness which characterized everything he did. He sat silent a moment, staring out the mow. Then he said, 'Suppose they don't come at us across the creek? Suppose they sweep down the valley instead? Can we stop a mounted charge?'

Donovan flushed. He should have thought of that himself. A bold frontal attack just might succeed in taking the house, with all their food, ammunition, water supply, and possibly the woman and the boy.

He wasn't concentrating.

He had to get his mind off the woman.

'We could stop it if we had an open field of fire from here.'

'We have,' Simpson said. 'I put in gun ports when I built this barn. Not so much against 'Paches as against horse thieves.'

'Then let's get them open.'

Within minutes, a cool cross current of air was blowing through the gun ports.

60

Donovan peered out across the day-bright meadow. Nothing could move across those five hundred yards without being spotted. He looked at Simpson. Fatigue drew the man's head down upon his chest. It was obvious he hadn't slept while off watch.

Damn the woman! She was on Simpson's mind, too.

'You'd better go back to the house and get some sleep. You're going to have to be wide awake in a few hours.'

'I'm all right,' Simpson protested.

'If you closed your eyes for five minutes we could all be dead.'

'What about you? You've had no sleep in days.'

'I'm used to it by now.'

Simpson hesitated, looking at Donovan in awkward silence. At last he said, 'Peggy – my wife – wants me to send you away. Or turn you over to Delcha. She thinks that then the Apaches would go away and leave us alone.'

Donovan chewed thoughtfully on a piece of straw. 'What did you tell her?'

'That I couldn't do it.'

'She'll not be satisfied with that.'

'I know.'

'Well, she's your problem,' Donovan said. 'Just keep her out of my hair.'

Half way down the ladder, Simpson paused. 'I can't even promise that,' he said. 'My wife seems to be the one thing I can't control.'

With a shrug, Donovan turned back to the creek-side window. Simpson's wife trouble was his own affair.

If she became his, he would know how to handle her.

'Peggy!'

She came instantly awake, her heart hammering with terror. And then she heard Pete rapping on the door and the fear went out of her. In the three years of their marriage, she had never before locked him out. Well, there was always a first time.

'What do you want, Pete?'

'The door's locked.'

'I know.'

'Peggy, don't act like a child!'

Her mouth tightened. 'What time is it?'

'It's midnight.'

'There's quilts and a pillow on the chair beside the stove,' she said. 'Wake me when it's time.'

She heard him cross the room and then the scuff of boots as he stretched out on his pallet. She lay quietly waiting, aware that only a few feet away he was staring up into the darkness, torn by emotions just as she was. Only he was thinking of her. She was thinking of Donovan. She had to see him, to try and get him to leave before they were all killed. Or before he closed her into an even tighter trap.

It was half an hour before Pete's breathing changed and she was sure he was asleep. Throwing back the covers, she pulled on her boots, and fully dressed, went into the other room. Pete was a dark shadow on the floor near the window. She opened the door and slipped quietly into the night.

Sprawled on his belly, rifle within easy reach, Donovan swept the deep shadowed timber beyond the creek for signs of movement. Surrounded by the enemy and with no real hope of escape, he was, paradoxically, more relaxed than he had been in weeks. He was through running. Whether he willed it or not, his fate was now irrevocably linked with three people.

A quiet man who loved a wife who neither loved nor respected him.

A beautiful woman tormented by a river of fire coursing through her magnificent body.

A spoiled fourteen year old kid who despised his stepfather as an intruder and a weakling and, unconsciously, resented his mother for having entered into the marriage.

Already he had glimpsed the dark, just below the surface frictions which lacerated their minds. The woman's mixed-up fear of him, the boy's hatred for him, and Pete Simpson's held back resentment.

Simpson and the boy he could handle.

It was the woman who was unpredictable.

Quick to sense the empathy between Donovan and herself, she was now afraid of what he might do to her life. The moment she felt her little world collapsing around her, she would, in her terror, stop at nothing to destroy him. Cornered, she would kill...

A horse whickered outside.

Donovan reached for the Winchester.

In the corral, the horse herd stood bunched quietly hip-shot or with their necks resting on one another's rumps.

Donovan remained motionless, waiting. Something moved in the shadows near the corral. He snapped up the rifle.

Fifty feet away, Peggy Simpson slipped into the clearing.

Donovan lowered the Winchester.

The woman paused. 'Donovan?' she called softly.

'What's wrong?'

'I want to talk to you.'

A moment later, he heard her moving about in the darkness below and then the faint scrape of her boots on the ladder.

Climbing into the mow, she straightened, brushing hay from her hair and dress. Moonlight slanted in and laid full across her sullen features.

'You fool!' Donovan said harshly. 'Do you realize I almost shot you?'

Her mouth shaped itself into a bitter line. 'It might have been better if you had. Instead of what you're doing to me.'

He understood her meaning but chose to ignore it. 'Why did you come? Don't you realize what will happen if your husband finds you here?'

He saw the quick rise and fall of her breasts and knew that she was under great emotional stress.

'That's why you've got to leave,' she said. *'Now, tonight.'*

'You're out of your mind!' he retorted. 'The place is surrounded.'

'Just the same you've got to leave.'

Donovan propped the rifle against the wall. 'Do you know what Apaches do to a man who kills one of their blood brothers? They stake him out in the sun with rawhide around his throat, cut off his eyelids, slit open his belly and fill it with sand – and then sit in a circle and watch him die. A strong man can take a long time dying that way.'

Peggy Simpson wet her lips, hesitated, then lifted her chin defiantly. 'I don't care! I'll not risk my life for a damn bounty hunter!'

Donovan's face settled into an impassive mould. 'What have you got against bounty hunters?'

'I'll tell you what!' she flared. 'One of them brought in my first husband for the law to hang!'

'Men hang themselves,' Donovan retorted. 'But if you've got to blame somebody, blame the judge and jury.'

Like a slow burning fuse, Peggy Simpson's anger reached the powder keg of her mind and exploded.

'Don't preach to me, damn you!' she screamed. 'If you don't get off this place now, tonight, I'll kill you! I told Pete I would and I will!'

Anger made her even more beautiful and Donovan felt the heat rise in him. She did that to men, he thought. Too many men for her own good. And still they couldn't put out the fire in her.

'Why don't you stop acting like a fool,' he said, 'and go back to your husband.'

He put his back to her and moved away.

It was a mistake that almost cost him his life.

The *snick* of the Winchester being hand-cocked spun him around.

She had the rifle to her shoulder, her finger on the trigger. He heard the hammer fall and braced himself for the smack of the bullet, and when it did not come he remembered that he had forgotten to jack a shell into the chamber – and then he crashed into her and the two of them went tumbling back into the sweet smelling hay and she lay there, her breasts heaving against her tightly stretched bodice and the softness of her belly under his hand and her eyes growing bigger and bigger and her whole body vibrating and the full lips parting and, at last, a tormented moan torn from her as she arched upward to meet his thrust.

'Damn you, Donovan!' she cried. 'Damn you for a... *Ah, Donovan!'*

Frantically, she wrapped her arms around the doll, drawing it to her, holding it close, gaining comfort from its warmth and not feeling lonely anymore but safe and secure and good.

Ah, so good!

Squeezing the doll to her breasts, she cried out in ecstasy as a great pulsing flow of love filled her, lifting her up, higher and higher, until somewhere out in the beauty of space her strength failed and she fell, spinning, back to earth.

And then, as always, the doll was gone and she was lying there in the hay, staring up into the raftered darkness, with the moonlight slanting across her face and the old loneliness, the emptiness bearing down upon her once more.

Where had the doll gone? And why could she find it only in men's arms? What had happened to the doll? Who had taken it from her?

She had long since forgotten who had given her the doll. Aunt Jessica perhaps after the death of her own child. Or it might have been some invalided soldier passing through Kansas on his way home from the war. Sometimes, a sweeter memory skittered around the fringes of her memory, but she could never quite capture it. What she most vividly remembered was that whoever had given her the doll had loved her. She had known that from the moment she had first hugged the sawdust packed body with its shoe-button eyes and painted smile to her.

Until that moment, she had never had a

single thing in her life that she could call her own. A Baptist minister's salary in Lawrence, Kansas made no allowances for personal possessions. Especially a minister whose wife bore him a child with monotonous regularity every year for seventeen years, and managed to keep eight of them alive.

Even such simple necessities as shoes or a dress did not really *belong* to one; there was always a 'next-in-line' waiting to take them away when they became too small. And a bit of ribbon, a few inches of cheap lace, or a brightly colored sash were dismissed as 'useless, expensive symbols of female vanity and sinful pride'.

'No daughter of mine is going to rob the Lord's coffers for barbaric self-glorification,' the Reverend Herman Wolke had vowed and, until the day he died, he had rigidly upheld that view.

As the first born, Peggy had been a deep source of disappointment to her parents. She 'should have been a boy' – as though she had been granted some mysterious power of choice and had personally failed them. That resentment carried over through the years as Sarah Wolke produced one girl after another. Herman Wolke blamed the tragedy upon his wife who, in turn, declared it was God's punishment upon him for his 'unholy lusts of the flesh'. Both secretly considered it a painful symbol of their collective failure in life.

Other than this resentful 'recognition' of her existence, Herman Wolke ignored his eldest daughter as, for that matter, he did all his incredible brood. God had ordered that Man should propagate and, as a servant of the Lord, he did his duty with, as some people observed, 'remarkable enthusiasm'. Upon the birth of the child, however, his sense of duty waned, and from there on, Sarah Wolke, a shrill-voiced, domineering woman, took over.

As a hell's-fire-and-brimstone preacher, Herman Wolke was a success. That is if success meant crowding his church every Sabbath with people who sometimes wondered whether God, the Devil, or Herman Wolke was to be the most feared.

As a man, he was a complete failure, envious of the power, the prestige, and the affluence of his congregation even while he ranted against the evils of materialism.

As a father, he was a cold, harsh voice and a heavy hand. A man without warmth, affection, or love for anything but God, and Peggy often felt that he took a secret pleasure in

dwelling upon the cruelty and petty jea-
lousies of the wrathful Jehovah whom he
served. Certainly he tried to emulate his
master in his unforgiving judgments upon
others. Of Jesus Christ he spoke but seldom
if at all, or of the love which Christ enjoined
men to have for one another.

Love was an alien word to the Reverend
Herman Wolke and to his household.

And to Peggy Wolke until the doll entered
her life.

She was twelve at the time. Old for a girl
to be playing with dolls, but not for one who
had never owned a doll in her life. Not for a
girl whose whole existence had been one of
almost complete isolation, cut off as she was
by her father's bigotry from the rest of the
children of Lawrence.

Nor did she share anything in common
with the family. Her father she avoided as
much as possible. Her mother also, after
being repeatedly repulsed as a 'sentimental
creature always craving affection'. In some
ways, an almost *unnatural* child.

Actually, the only thing unnatural about
her was that she wanted love in a household
where love was a stranger. Even her sisters
were remote, withdrawn, as though their
humanism had been destroyed during the

71

fetal stage.

In her loneliness, she created a world of her own and retreated into it when she could no longer bear the reality. Had she not been able to escape periodically to the prairie country outside Lawrence she might never have emerged from her world of make-believe.

But lying on her stomach beneath the great cottonwood down by the creek, with meadow larks flashing across the blue, cloud-puffed sky and the sea of grass rippling in the wind, Peggy Wolke dreamed of another world where men lived the things they believed in, rather than preached them. Where people loved one another because it was not only the right thing to do, it was the sensible thing. For where there was love and laughter in a man's heart good things just naturally came to him. But when a man hated as her father did he stirred up hate in other people and bad things happened to him and his soul dried up and he was no good to anybody, least of all to God.

Dominating her dreams was the firm conviction that someday, someone would come into her world who was not afraid to love. Who would not think that wanting to touch someone to show that you cared was 'unnatural', and who would make her forget the loneliness that was always with her.

And so she dreamed until the doll came into her life.

From that moment, everything changed. She was no longer alone. Now she had a friend whom she could love and who, most wonderful of all, loved her. *Two* friends. The doll and the one who had given it to her, although she was *never* able to remember anything about this 'one' save a strong, brown hand – she thought it was a man's – stretched out, offering the doll. Later, she was to realize that she had deliberately obliterated the donor's identity because she had not wanted the doll given to her. It had come to her of its own accord. It had come to her because it loved her.

And so she and the doll had talked and played and shared their secrets, and eaten and slept together for almost three years.

Until that day when...

No! No! No!

She began to cry.

Lying relaxed beside her, Donovan wondered what madness had made him forget the Apaches out there in the night while he made love to another man's wife.

He felt no sense of having betrayed Pete

Simpson. He barely knew the man. The woman, however, was another matter. He had believed her to be merely a hot-blooded slut. He had been wrong. Peggy Simpson was a tormented woman, desperately seeking something she had lost, but not finding it in strange men's arms.

'Tell me,' he said quietly. 'Why do you do it when you really don't enjoy it?'

A little sigh escaped her. 'I don't know,' she said. 'I've thought about it a lot. I guess maybe it's because for a few minutes it makes me feel...'

'Loved?'

'I suppose that's it.'

'But it never lasts, does it?'

'No. But I always keep hoping it will.'

Drawing her to him, Donovan pressed her head against his shoulder. 'Tell me about yourself.'

'You'd never understand.'

'I might.'

Slowly, painfully, it came out of her, as though even the remembering hurt. And, listening, Donovan began to gradually understand the forces which had moulded her and from which she sought to escape.

A home in which love had been a stranger. A fanatic, fundamentalist minister-father who had preached about a God whom he had never known. Who had hated his 'sheep' and enjoyed frightening them with threats of hell's fires while he lived in a secret hell of his own making.

A strong, domineering mother who had hated her own sex as weak, foolish creatures, her role as mother, and her daughters, especially Peggy, for 'not being sons'.

Seven warped sisters with whom Peggy had had nothing in common.

A complete isolation from other children.

And shielding her from these forces, a doll given her by someone she either couldn't or wouldn't remember. As long as she'd had the doll she had been able to survive. But then something had happened, and she had begun her desperate search to find someone to take the doll's place.

She could have stopped there and Donovan would have understood. He'd known other women like her. Women who had lost sweethearts, husbands, or children and who had tried to fill the vacuum with physical love.

'What happened to the doll?' he asked.

'Quantrill burned her to death.' Peggy Simpson's voice was remote, trance-like. She was still wandering around in some shadowy land between past and present. 'Along with my parents, all my sisters, and half the town.'

'Quantrill burned her?'

'Yes. He and his guerrillas rode into Lawrence and burned and raped and looted. I hid out under the big cottonwood down by the creek and they missed me. After they left, I went back and people were still lying in the streets unburied, and stores and the church were burned down and my father and mother and my sisters dead inside.

'Then I went home, or where home had been, and tried to find Dianne, that was the doll's name. People tried to take me away but I wouldn't leave. I hunted through the ashes all day. I never found her. *I ... never ... found ... her!* Not even one of her little shoe-button eyes!'

She sucked in her breath with a low, child-like whimper, then suddenly rolled over and, pressing her face to Donovan's chest, gave way to all her pent-up sorrow and loneliness.

'Oh, damn you, Donovan!' she cried. 'No one ever knew about the doll! Not even Monty.'

'Monty?'

'Monty Lord, my first husband.'

Donovan's face darkened. *Monty Lord!* No wonder the boy Tommy had reminded him of someone. He mirrored his father. Except that he had shown courage against the Apaches. Something his father had not done when Donovan had cornered him in a dirty little *cantina* in Sonora.

Remembering, Donovan wondered what a beautiful, intelligent woman like Peggy Simpson could have seen in a man who would drop down on his knees and beg ... beg, by God, with twenty peons looking on ... for his freedom. What would happen to her cherished dreams if she knew that Monty had offered her as a bribe to try and buy that freedom?

His arm tightened around her. 'Why didn't you tell Monty about the doll?'

She raised her head and looked at him, bitter-eyed. 'First you rape me. Now you invade my mind and tear open my heart. You know why I didn't tell him. He would have laughed at me. He wasn't the kind to understand women.

'He thought I slept with other men to pay off his gambling debts because I loved him. He was wrong. I did it because I couldn't help myself. I was hunting the doll, Donovan. I've been hunting the doll all my life, only I didn't realize it until tonight.'

'Did you love Monty Lord?'

'I thought I did,' she said slowly. 'Now I know that he simply happened to be the first man to show me attention after Quantrill's raid. I was sixteen, alone, and without the doll to love me anymore. For years, I pretended that Monty was the doll. Only he wasn't. If he had been, I wouldn't have gone to other men.'

Propping herself on her elbows, she studied Donovan with a grave expression.

'You're the first since I married Pete. If he and I hadn't quarreled over you, this might not have happened. I don't know. Yes, I do. I knew from the very beginning. That's why I wanted you to leave. I was afraid that if you lit me I'd never be able to put out the fire again. It's a nightmare I've lived with all my life. Do you think I'm a whore, Donovan?'

'No.'

She laid her head back on his shoulder with a little sigh. 'Maybe that was why I told you about the doll. I knew you would understand.'

Donovan felt her breasts flatten against his chest.

'I've never known anyone like you before,' she said. 'It's almost as if you were a part of me. You make me feel safe and warm and secure. No man's ever been able to do that before.

'The others made me feel like a slut. With you, it was different. I felt ashamed, but only for a little while. Suddenly, it all seemed somehow right and beautiful. Do you know why?' She turned her head and looked at Donovan.

'Because you're different. No matter what else you are, you care for people. You care for me. Maybe not as a woman, but as a human being.' She caught her breath. 'Please, Donovan, don't hurt me. I don't think I can stand being hurt anymore.'

With a low moan, she came to him. 'Make love to me, Donovan. Make me forget...'

'Ma! Pete! Donovan! Help me! Hel–'

Thinned by terror, Tommy Lord's voice cut through the night and then shut off abruptly.

'Oh, my God!' Peggy Simpson rolled away from Donovan. She was on her feet, pulling her dress on over her head as she ran toward the ladder.

'No!' Donovan grabbed her. 'You go out there now and they'll riddle you.'

'Don't you understand?' she cried. 'They've got Tommy!'

A rifle cracked twice in rapid succession.

'Damn you!' Peggy Simpson tried frantically to break away. *'Let me go!'*

'Stop it!' Donovan shook her roughly. 'Getting yourself killed won't help him.'

'Donovan, he's only a boy!'

'I know that. And I'll do...'

'Donovan!' Simpson shouted from the cabin. 'They've got Peggy and Tommy!'

There was no way of keeping it a secret. 'Your wife is here with me.'

After a long pause, Simpson answered in a strained voice. 'Is Tommy there, too?'

'No.'

A pause. 'Peggy?'

'Yes, Pete?'

'I'm going after him.'

'They'd kill you before you reached the creek!' Donovan shouted. 'If the boy's still alive they'll not harm him before morning. By then maybe we can figure out a way to help him.'

'Peggy?'

'Donovan's right, Pete.'

'It's your decision.' After that, Simpson did not speak again.

Picking up his rifle, Donovan moved to the mow window. 'Here.' He drew Peggy down beside him. 'Try and get some sleep.'

She stretched out with a weary little sigh.

'I can't sleep.'

'Then try and rest. It's going to be a rough day.'

'Will they torture him?'

'They'll use him to try and force me out.'

'I don't think I can stand that.' She sat up. 'If I hadn't come out here it wouldn't have happened.'

'You don't know that. The boy probably heard something and slipped outside to check. That's when they caught him.'

'But if I'd been there...'

'He didn't wake Pete. He wouldn't have awakened you.'

She seemed to derive some comfort from the thought, and Donovan felt a little of the tenseness go out of her.

'What will you do if they torture him?'

'Whatever has to be done.'

'Donovan, do you think we'll live through this?'

He studied the creek for a long time. 'I don't know, Peggy. I just don't know.'

'Can I stay here with you? I mean – I don't want to die alone. And I'd be alone if I were with Pete.'

'Stay if you want.'

Her head fell back on his shoulder and he could smell the clean fragrance of her hair.

She said quietly, 'Pete knows about us.'

'How could he?'

'He knew the minute you told him I was up here with you.'

'But he doesn't know that the real reason you came up here was to kill me. You did try, you know.'

She shook her head. 'Pete senses things even before they happen. I told him I intended to find me another man when this was over. I think he guessed even then I was hunting an excuse to come to you.'

'Then he'll want to settle with me.'

'He hasn't got the guts,' Peggy Simpson said bitterly.

'You underestimate him,' Donovan replied. 'He'll take a lot. But when he's had his fill, watch out.'

'You like him, don't you?'

'He's got character.'

'And me?'

'You've got too much idealism in your make-up,' Donovan told her. 'You need to stop dreaming and start living.'

She closed her eyes and listened to the sound of the creek. Somewhere out there in the darkness, a terrified fourteen-year-old boy was sweating out the hours while she lay here talking, her emotions all mixed up with this man beside her.

'Donovan...' drowsily. 'You won't let them torture him, will you?'

'No.'

No more than he can stand. Or I can stand.

'Donovan...' The rushing sound of the creek was growing fainter. 'You're a fantastic man.'

And then she was asleep.

Gently, Donovan lowered her to the hay. For a long time, he sat studying her with thoughtful eyes. Then he remembered the boy Tommy and what he, Donovan, would have to do before the coming day was over.

For Tommy Lord the hours past midnight were a nightmare. Shortly after one o'clock he had awakened from a fitful sleep and lain there in the darkness, listening, his heart hammering in his chest. From the front room he could hear the sound of Pete's exhausted breathing and wondered why his stepfather wasn't in the bedroom.

And then out there in the meadow he heard it again. The hoot of an owl. The thudding of his heart eased. Damned owl! He burrowed into his pillow and started to drift off again.

Owl!

83

He snapped up in bed, wide awake, trembling. He hadn't heard an owl in the meadow since him an' Ma had been here.

Quickly he rose and slipped on his boots. Carrying his rifle, he went into the front room. Pete lay on a pallet near the window. The bedroom door was closed.

So Pete an' Ma had had an argument. That should have pleased him, but it didn't. He couldn't forget how Pete had lied in his teeth to spare his pride. Pete hadn't had to do that.

Standing there in the dark, listening to the hoot of an owl that wasn't really an owl out there in the meadow, he wasn't nearly so scared with Pete lying there on the pallet, his Winchester beside him.

About to wake Pete, he changed his mind. Like Pete had said, it was time he started acting like a man. Heck, if it was a 'Pache out there he'd just squeeze off a shot an' high-tail it back to the house. There was nothin' to be scared of. Well, almost nothin'.

As he moved past the bedroom, he noticed the door was slightly ajar. A thin strip of moonlight glowed through the crack. He paused. Ma just might be awake. Maybe he ought to tell her about the owl.

'Ma!'

Pete stirred restlessly on the pallet.

'Ma!' He pushed the door open and stuck his head inside.

And then he saw the empty bed, the thrown back covers, and a new terror seized him. He was young but he was no fool. If it had been 'Paches they would all be dead. An' Ma wouldn't have risked going to the privy; she'd have used the chamber pot. Had she heard the owl, too, an' gone out to check? No, she'd have woke him or Pete.

Then why had she gone out without telling...

Donovan! His mother an' Donovan! An' with Pete lying over there on a pallet, trusting her!

He leaned against the door, sick, scared and angry, remembering the way Donovan had looked at his mother, an' how she had acted when Donovan was around. She'd pretended to hate the big bastard an' maybe she thought she did until her an' Pete quarreled.

Dammit, why'd she have to hurt Pete that way? Maybe he wasn't much, but when you stopped to think about it he'd been pretty good to them. 'Course, she couldn't help not loving Pete. But right was right an' wrong was wrong, an' what her an' Donovan were doing up there in the hay wasn't right.

A sense of loss bore heavily upon him. These past few hours he'd begun to understand Pete a lot better. He'd even hoped that someday they might be able to hit it off.

Now *this!*

Pete was bound to find out. When he did there would be hell to pay. Pete wouldn't stand for a woman cheating on him. An' you sure couldn't fault him for that.

The thought brought on a new terror. Maybe Ma had decided not to stick around an' get throwed out. Maybe she'd already cut out with Donovan. If anybody could slip past them 'Paches, Donovan could. The big, mean son of a bitch! He half hoped Delcha caught the bastard and castrated him. That would put a stop to his philanderin'!

Tommy hesitated, undecided as to what to do now. He had forgotten the owl out there in the meadow. His only thought was to find his Ma before it was too late.

Slipping outside, he worked his way through the deep shadows toward the corral.

Halfway there, an owl hooted softly twenty feet to his right.

He stopped, swinging up the Winchester. His heart hammered. A big cotton ball filled his throat. He couldn't swallow. He couldn't make spit.

He was still standing there, listening, when Delcha and Pena came at him out of the night.

He screamed, 'Ma! Pete! Donovan!' and tried to bring the rifle to bear. 'Help me! Hel–'

A savage blow to the head knocked him senseless.

Slinging the boy across his shoulder, Delcha faded back across the meadow with Pena running close behind him.

A rifle cracked from the cabin and a bullet whizzed past Delcha's head. Again. The slug passed cleanly through Pena's leg. He stumbled, caught himself and kept running.

Circling, Delcha and Pena entered the timber from the west. In a small clearing, fourteen braves lay sprawled on the ground sleeping. While Pena tended his wound, Delcha trussed up his still unconscious captive. Then he stretched out on his back and smiled up at the high-riding moon.

The White Eyes had led them over a long, crooked trail. He was a brave man, this White Eyes, but he was not an Apache. He could not watch a friend die in agony. When the sun got hot and the rawhides started to shrink and the boy began to scream, the White Eyes would come for him.

He, Delcha, would be waiting.

The coffee pot was empty.

Pete Simpson shrugged. He'd had enough. That was all he'd done for the past two hours – drink coffee and think. And still he couldn't reconcile himself to the truth.

Peggy and Donovan!

Donovan he could understand. Big, virile, with strong physical appetites. A woman like Peggy was bound to arouse such a man.

But Peggy!

As Monty Lord's wife she had slept with many men. Tucson gossip said that Monty had made her do it to pay off his gambling debts. Others vowed that she was nothing but an out and out whore. He, Pete, had believed neither. Whatever it was that drove her to men's arms, it was not Monty Lord nor mere physical passion.

During the past four years, many men had come to the ranch on business. A few, after seeing Peggy, had returned with more social pleasures in mind. Some, while he was away. But until Donovan had ridden into their lives, she had never once betrayed him. This he knew with the same intuitive certainty that he now knew she had slept with Donovan.

The past had begun to fade. She had changed. The fire had started to cool in her. Now Donovan had lit it again.

That Donovan had bedded her did not matter so much. He could forgive that. It was the thought that he had driven her to it that tormented Pete Simpson. If he'd sent Donovan away like she wanted him to, nothing would have happened. But she'd sworn she'd get herself another man, and she had. But why Donovan? She hated the man.

Time.

Time was running out on them. Peggy knew it. They all knew it. She might never have another chance, and she was not going to be cheated of her revenge. Donovan was male, handy, and he, Pete, was just going to have to stand by and take it.

Simpson winced. Did she really think him that weak, that lacking in self-respect? Didn't she realize that he would have no choice but to settle with Donovan? In a gun fight he wouldn't have a chance. Did she really hate him bad enough to want him killed?

He couldn't believe it of her. He would rather think it a simple case of passion running away with reason. That he could understand and, in time, forgive. But to want him dead...

Opening the door, he stepped outside, letting the crisp air cool his heated brain. Dawn was lightening the sky to the east. Trees, corral posts, the barn, and the woodshed had started to take on definite shape.

Everything slept, even the earth. It was that hour when life reached its lowest ebb. When men died quietly in their sleep, or violently at one another's hands.

His breath went out with a sudden gust. *Damn!* Why had he destroyed his life for the sake of a man he'd known only a few hours? A man who'd shown his gratitude by sleeping with his benefactor's wife. Or perhaps his contempt for a husband who couldn't hold her to begin with.

Goddammit, why?

Carrying his rifle, he walked around to the back of the house. There was no sign of life from the barn. Were they up there in the hay making love again? Had either of them given a thought to Tommy, somewhere out there in the timber going through God knew what kind of torment?

He was one to talk! If he'd been awake as he should have been, the thing would never have happened. It was not hard to guess

Tommy's actions. The boy had heard something outside to investigate. He'd run smack into a couple of 'Pache probably bent upon running off the horses.

It was the last straw, Simpson thought. If he had not lost Peggy before, he had lost her now. She would never forgive him if they tortured the boy to death.

But the worst punishment would come from himself. He knew why Tommy hadn't awakened him.

You've been trying to act like a man for the past year. Bitter, sarcastic. *Now start being one. You may never have another chance.*

As long as he lived those words would torment him. For that was exactly what Tommy had tried to do. Act like a man.

Damn!

From atop the woodshed a rooster crowed lustily, and from somewhere he heard the mournful cry of a dove. Gradually, the Mazatals were beginning to stand up against the skyline.

Simpson's mouth tightened. Any moment now 'Paches would slip out of the timber, not yipping and screaming like Sioux, Cheyenne or Arapahoe, but silently because 'Paches didn't scalp or count coup. They just liked to torture and kill.

91

A horse whickered in the corral.

Simpson levered a shell into the Winchester.

Out in the meadow, an owl hooted and in a moment a second answered from the timber.

'Look out, Donovan!' Simpson yelled. 'They're in the timber!'

'I heard them,' Donovan answered instantly from the barn. 'Get back inside!'

Simpson backed into the room and bolted the door. From the window, he watched the meadow and the lightening sky beyond.

Watched and waited.

Kneeling at the mow window, Peggy Simpson cocked the long-barreled, single-action Colt. She was scared. More scared than she had been during the first attack. That had come in mid-afternoon when she could relate to things. But lying here staring out into the weird half light which made even familiar things seem somehow strange and alien, listening for the faint splash of water that would tell her they had crossed the creek, she knew an unreasoning terror.

She looked toward Donovan and just the sight of him washed away her fear. As long as he was there, massive, implacable, nothing could harm her.

Reassured, she turned back to the window.

At the gun port, Donovan frowned. It was not like Apaches to risk an attack when they had the bait to flush their quarry.

Was the boy Tommy dead?

Peggy Simpson must have sensed his concern. 'You said they wouldn't attack!' she cried. 'You said they'd try to force you out!'

'It seems I was wrong,' Donovan said. 'They're in a killing mood.'

The woman's face darkened. Although she had recognized the possibility of death, she had never accepted it as inevitable. Until this moment, she had firmly believed that, if there was no other way, Donovan would give himself up. And that the Apaches would simply ride away and leave them alone.

Now Donovan had destroyed that illusion.

Anger replaced the warmth she had felt for him only moments before.

'You've as good as murdered us all! Why...'

'*Shut up!*'

Something had moved out there in the darkness. For a moment, Donovan lost track of it. Then he picked it up again ten yards closer.

'Look out, Simpson,' he yelled, and fired. 'Here they come!'

The shadow leaped high against the sky and died.

Out of the grass they came, five of them, wide-spread and moving fast.

From the cabin, Simpson opened up, dropping one of them. Still they came, bent low and running a zig-zag pattern that, in the dim light, made them difficult targets.

'The creek!' Peggy Simpson cried from the window. 'They're crossing the creek!'

By the time Donovan joined her it was too late. Delcha's main party had already crossed over. Flashes of gunfire winked palely from outbuildings and from behind the big oak in the yard.

Delcha's strategy was obvious. If he could split the defenders he would then be able to launch simultaneous attacks against both barn and cabin. With the odds seven or eight to one, neither man would be able to help the other. Simpson's position was already critical. Unless he got fire support quickly he would be overrun.

'Watch the window, Peggy!'

He ran back to the gun port.

From the cabin he could hear the steady crack of Simpson's rifle. But already a couple of Apaches had managed to close in from the rear. One was working his way along the wall near the back door. Another crouched beneath the kitchen window, rifle at the ready.

Donovan killed the one beneath the window. The other faded back into the darkness.

Suddenly, in the corral, horses began to neigh and to race about in confusion.

'My God, they're after the horses!' Peggy Simpson cried, and opened fire.

Donovan leaped back to the window.

An Apache, waving a white shirt, was driving the herd toward the half-open gate.

A belly-shot pitched him forward, and the herd swung back to the far side of the corral.

Reloading, Donovan ran back to the gun port. Dark figures slipping from tree to tree, building to building, working steadily closer.

Donovan waited.

As dawn spilled over the Rim, Delcha launched a three-pronged attack against cabin, barn and horse herd. Bullets thudded into the barn walls and splintered the shake roof. Donovan fired as fast as he could, but in the dim light could not be certain if he scored any hits.

Rushing to cover his own rear, Simpson pinned down two raiders behind the big oak in the yard.

Donovan could not stop the creek-side attack.

As Delcha's party swept inside the barn, he stood at the ladder and emptied his rifle into the darkness below. A mare in foal neighed in terror and began kicking at the sides of her stall. A man screamed. Then gun flame gouted and Donovan went down as a bullet trenched his leg from knee to hip.

Peggy Simpson turned a pale face toward him. 'Oh, my God! Are you hit bad?'

'No,' Donovan said. Then in a low, calm voice: *'Don't move.'*

Standing on a ladder beneath the mow window, the Apache had his elbows hooked on the mow floor and his rifle aimed, when Donovan's slug knocked him out into space.

'I told you to watch that window!'

Tight lipped, Peggy Simpson crawled over to him. 'Give me your knife.'

Expertly, she slit the trouser leg to the hip, exposing the long, ugly wound. It was deep and bleeding freely. She bound the wound with strips torn from her petticoat.

'That should take care of it.'

'Thanks.' Donovan smiled briefly. 'You

don't need a doll. You don't need anyone.'

He was on his feet when the second Apache tried to heave himself into the mow. Donovan snapped off a shot at point blank range.

The bullet passed cleanly through the Apache's chest. Blood gushed from his mouth. For a moment, he hung there on his forearms, his widespread fingers pressing against the floor in a desperate effort to hold on. Then, slowly, the fingers relaxed and he fell backwards off the ladder.

Firing broke out everywhere, with bullets snapping up through the floor boards and filling the air with flying splinters. The mow was becoming a death trap.

Donovan limped back to the gun port, feeling the pain flow hot and wet down his thigh. Their position had now become un-tenable. If he lost consciousness the woman would not have a chance. Nor, isolated in the cabin, would Simpson.

Delcha had to be cleared out of the barn, and quickly. If Simpson could get close enough to use the Greener and with him firing from above, it just might be done.

About to call out from Simpson, he caught a flick of movement behind the big oak and knew that he might as well forget it.

It was a Mexican stand-off.

The Apaches behind the tree couldn't reach the cabin. Simpson couldn't reach the barn. In the barn, Donovan and Peggy Simpson could neither leave nor stay.

The woman would have to try it alone.

Checking his rifle, Donovan jerked his head toward the window. 'Get going!'

Peggy Simpson did not answer him immediately, but lay atop the hay studying him with a sullen resentment. Until she had seen his blood flowing freely between her fingers, she had believed him indestructible, and, so believing, had felt safe, secure. For a few brief hours, he had permitted her to hope and dream of a day when she could forget the shame, the sorrow and the loneliness that had been her entire life. Then incredibly, through some incalculable error on his part, he had been at the wrong place at the wrong time. And in that single bloody instant, he had destroyed her invincibility and her dream.

Looking at him, she experienced a sense of personal outrage, as though by the act he had deliberately and cruelly hurt her. She had thought him different; he wasn't. He was like all the others who had let her down – Pete, Monty, and all the faceless, sweaty bodies with whom she had shared a moment's loveless passion.

'Goddammit,' Donovan snapped. 'I said get going!'

She regarded him coldly. 'I'll make up my own mind from now on. I don't need you anymore.'

'You never needed me.' The big man smiled grimly. *'Now, move!'*

She slid off the hay. 'What about you?'

'I'll cover you from here.'

'Oh, no!' she retorted. 'I'll not owe you my life twice. We'll go out of here together, or we don't go.'

Their eyes locked, clashed briefly, then Donovan shrugged. 'I haven't got time to argue with you.' He put his face to the gun port and shouted, 'Simpson!'

'Yeah?'

'I'm going to flush those two bucks behind the tree. You pick them off. Then cover the barn door with the Greener. You're likely to get some action.'

'Okay. Go ahead.'

Over his shoulder, Donovan ordered, 'Down you go, Peggy.'

'Donovan...'

'Move!'

Sullenly, she obeyed.

99

With a methodical precision, Donovan 'barked' the two Apaches around the tree like squirrels until they came into Pete Simpson's gunsight.

Caught in a cross-fire, they broke cover and dashed for the woodshed. One made it; one didn't.

Back once more to the ladder, Donovan emptied his rifle into the darkness below. Then he ran to the window.

Peggy Simpson was gone.

Donovan straddled the ladder and slid down. He jumped the last three feet, his wounded leg buckling as he hit the ground. He was still on his knees, the empty Winchester in his hand, when Peggy killed her first Apache.

The shot both betrayed them and saved them.

Pouring out of the barn to cut off Donovan's escape, Delcha's party caught both barrels of Pete Simpson's Greener. Two men died, shredded. Several others yelled in anguish. Demoralized, the survivors fled back across the creek and into the timber.

Giving Peggy Simpson a violent shove, Donovan yelled, *'Run!'*

She ran, with bullets pocking the ground around her all the way to the cabin.

From the cabin, Simpson gave Donovan a brisk supporting fire as he retreated slowly, matching shots with the frustrated Apaches across the creek. The last twenty feet Donovan covered on the run.

Inside, he dropped the heavy cross bar in place and turned.

The three of them stood there, observing one another warily, their breathing heavy in the silence. Pale dawn light flowed through the window and laid across their faces.

Two men and a woman bound together by a common urge for survival, yet ripped and torn by turbulent emotions which drove them from passionate love, deep resentments and a mounting hatred to the thin edge of murder.

From the beginning it had been a cumulative thing. Donovan had precipitated it. Peggy Simpson had complicated it. Simpson would, inevitably, try to terminate it.

This they all knew.

Donovan and the woman had candidly discussed the matter in the hay mow. Simpson had thought about it in the loneliness of the night. Now the knowledge had created an intolerable friction amongst them. A friction which, if they were to survive, would have to be pushed from their minds until they were free of this trap.

It was Donovan who broke the tension.

Limping into the kitchen, he dropped heavily onto a chair. He felt light-headed and sick at his stomach. He brushed a hand across his eyes and said to Simpson, 'You have any whiskey?'

'There's a bottle around someplace,' Simpson said. 'Peggy, will you see if you can find it?'

When she had gone, Simpson pulled up a chair and sat down. His face was grave.

'How bad are you hit?'

'I can still shoot.'

'For how long?'

'Long enough.' Donovan met the rancher's eyes steadily. 'They won't attack again. They'll torture the boy to try and draw me out.'

'My God!' Simpson paled. 'What are we going to do?'

'I don't know.'

'Hell, we just can't...' Simpson broke off as his wife returned with a pint bottle of whiskey.

Donovan drank a third of the bottle neat. It burned almost as much as the fire in his leg, but it cleared his mind. He took a deep breath.

'That's strong stuff on an empty stomach,' he said, and remembered that he had not eaten since the previous evening.

'Peggy, fix us some breakfast, will you? No telling when we'll have another chance to eat.'

Not until he saw the look on Simpson's face did he realize his mistake. It was not that he had used her name; it was the easy familiarity with which he had colored it.

He sat there holding the empty bottle and feeling sorry for Simpson. In the beginning, it had not mattered. If a man couldn't satisfy his wife but someone else could – well, that was the man's fault. Now he realized that the fault spread back over the years to parents who should have been born sterile, if they had to be born at all.

Pete Simpson was the unfortunate victim of circumstances over which he had no control.

Angered, Donovan thrust the thought aside. *Hell, all men were victims of circumstances, including himself. Hadn't his own nature driven him to create the situation which now threatened his life?*

It was tough about Simpson and his wife.

It was tough about young Tommy Lord. It was tough about him, Donovan. But then life itself was tough. A human jungle in which there was no place for sentiment.

To hell with Simpson's bruised...

'Pete, do you want me to cook something?'

Donovan looked up, startled.

Peggy Simpson stood facing her husband, the color high in her cheeks, letting him know that she was her own woman and still his wife, not Donovan's whore.

Tilting his chair, Simpson rocked gently back and forth, saying nothing. Perspiration stippled his forehead. His eyes were tormented.

Donovan hauled out the makings and rolled a cigarette. Still the silence held. He struck a match and studied Simpson over the yellow flame, remembering his first impression of the man.

Pete Simpson would ask, but he would not beg. Not for anything or anybody.

Unconsciously, perhaps, the woman had just set off another facet of his character.

There were times when Simpson would not ask – *period*. Not because of any false sense of pride, but out of a deep understanding of just such a situation as his wife had created.

In effect, this woman who had betrayed him only hours before was now saying, *'Pete, I'm willing to forgive and forget if you are. I'll do what you want, but you'll have to ask me first.'*

Simpson kept rocking. He understood her clearly enough. But in the past hour or so, the long dormant steel in his nature had begun to emerge. He was willing to forgive and, hopefully, to someday forget; the moment and the conditions, however, would be of his choosing, not hers.

'Pete!' Peggy Simpson's voice sharpened. 'I asked you a question!'

The rocking stopped.

'Why ask me?' Simpson said evenly. 'Donovan's told you what he wants. And haven't you been giving him everything he asks for? Hasn't she, Donovan?'

Touching the burned-down match to his cigarette, Donovan spoke calmly through the smoke.

'I'd say that was none of your business. A marriage license is not a bill of sale. Nor is a woman chattel, to be owned like a cow or a piece of furniture.'

He had no personal quarrel with Simpson, nor any desire to interfere in a family dispute. But Simpson's attitude had become quietly aggressive. To back away from him, under the circumstances, would be dangerous.

'Don't try and tell me about marriage,' Simpson retorted. 'Or how to deal with my wife.'

Donovan flicked out the match and exhaled slowly. 'Somebody needs to tell you. You don't seem to be having much success with either one. And talking to your wife as though she were a whore isn't going to help matters.'

The rancher flushed, aware that he had been placed in a poor light. His mouth set in a stubborn line. He looked at his wife.

'We'll eat later.'

It was an ultimatum.

Peggy Simpson met it head-on. Putting her back to her husband, she moved to the stove. She lit the wood laid in the fire-box, put on a pot of cold beans to warm and cut thick slices of bread. When the beans were warm, she filled a plate and set it before Donovan, along with a cup of coffee. Then resting her hand on his shoulder, she said with a studied coolness:

'If there's anything else you want, Donovan, all you have to do is ask for it.'

Her meaning was unmistakable.

Pete Simpson got up, poured himself a cup of coffee and drank it without haste. When he finished, he set the cup down and turned to his wife.

Until this moment, he had blamed himself for what had happened up there in the mow, and had been prepared to forgive in time. But she didn't want forgiveness. She wanted more revenge.

You bitch! he thought, but remained silent rather than let her know she had gotten to him.

He switched his attention to Donovan, who sat watching him with alert eyes.

'There's a limit to gratitude, Donovan. Remember that.'

He picked up his rifle and went into the front room, leaving Peggy standing there, her face dark with frustration.

'Damn him!' she said fiercely. *'Oh, damn him!'*

The burned-down cigarette seared Donovan's fingers. He ground it out in his plate and then said matter of factly, 'Why don't you swallow your pride and tell him you love him?'

'Love him?' Peggy Simpson stared at him. *'Love him!* My God, I hate his guts! I hope they kill him!'

'You may force me to do the job if you keep on needling him.'

The blue eyes flashed. 'And, damn you, too!'

She slammed into the bedroom.

Donovan stared thoughtfully at the closed door. She was going to make trouble. More perhaps than he could handle. Already she had pushed Simpson dangerously close to the breaking point.

This was the situation he had feared from the very beginning. Within less than twenty-four hours, the three of them were at one another's throats; and the real stress hadn't even begun.

Wait until Delcha went to work on the boy, Tommy.

That was when the woman would fragment.

That was when Pete Simpson might unwind.

That was when he, Donovan, would...

What would he do when the boy began to scream and beg?

He got up and went to the window overlooking the creek. The sun had started to shorten the shadows around the outbuildings and to reach out toward the timber. Somewhere back there, Delcha was plan-

108

ning his last desperate move. Down to less than a dozen warriors, the Apache would not risk another all-out attack.

From here on, it would be a battle of nerves.

Donovan swore softly.

Squatted on his haunches, Delcha morosely studied the half circle of faces around him. Three weeks ago, there had been twenty. Now there were eight. His friends in the Shadowland would not rest until the man who had sent them there was dead.

Delcha scowled. He was tired, physically and mentally. The long, relentless chase had burned the bright flame of vengeance down to a mere flicker. His missed the *rancheria,* the fiery *tiswin* and the heated thighs of his favorite squaw. In short, he yearned to follow his pony's tracks back to the White Mountains. If it were not for the White Eyes Donovan...

Donovan!

The name was bear's gall on his tongue, a bitterness spreading to his mind. So far, Donovan had outrun him, outfought him and outwitted him. Unless he killed the White Eyes soon, the young men would no longer follow him into battle, the young women would refuse to share his bed, and the old men would laugh him off the *rancheria*.

It was maddening to know that a man whom he had never seen at a range closer than five hundred yards should be able to do this to him, an Apache chief.

The White Eyes must die.

Thoughtfully, Delcha studied the tense, sullen faces about him. They, too, were tired of the chase. He could feel their hostility directed against him because of this last disastrous attack. His lip curled. They had short memories. He had argued against the move; but their blood had been up and they would not listen.

They would listen now.

His eyes ranged over them, challenging each in turn until they stared down at their moccasins. Only Pena refused to bow his head. He sat stolidly enduring the pain of his wound, his face filled with a sullen arrogance.

Delcha's lips flattened against his teeth. Pena had helped him to capture the young White Eyes. That had been a brave thing. But he had also argued in favor of the ill-fated attack. He would have to be watched in the future. He was not only headstrong;

110

he was ambitious.

This time he had made a mistake, and men had died. For a while, at least, his voice would be stilled. But the thirst for power would continue to drive him. Eventually, he would have to be dealt with.

Pena's face darkened. He knew what Delcha was thinking and it angered him that the man should read his mind so easily. His breath went out in an explosive grunt.

'So we failed,' he said. 'Now we do it your way.'

'Will that bring back our friends from the Shadowland?'

'It will avenge them.'

'What good is vengeance to the dead?'

Pena's eyes glowed but he kept his temper. 'And what good can come from warriors quarreling in battle?'

'Perhaps it will teach the fool to heed wise counsel,' Delcha retorted. Jumping to his feet, he gestured impatiently toward the young White Eyes.

'No more talk! We act now. You, Bestinez! Carry the boy.'

The eight arose, shouting their approval, and Delcha knew that he held them once more in the palm of his hand.

'Where do we do it?' Pena asked.

'In the meadow,' Delcha said. 'Where the White Eyes can see and hear.'

Rifle held loosely, he trotted off among the pinons, carefully working his way westward.

Bestinez, a stocky, powerful man, threw the still bound boy over his shoulder and followed, with the others close behind.

For a moment, Pena hesitated. Then sullenly he put his moccasins in the tracks of those ahead.

Head down across the Apache's shoulders, Tommy Lord tried to focus his mind upon what was happening. But a terror-filled night, plus hunger and exhaustion, had so dulled his senses that he was only half aware of his predicament.

Unable to sleep because of the cruel bite of the rawhide bindings, he had sweated out the long hours of darkness, waiting for the rescue that he was sure would come. When it did not, anger had interlaced his mounting fear. An unreasoning anger which fed upon deep-seated resentments.

He'd always said Pete Simpson was a weakling. Well, this proved it. No *real* man would let a bunch of mangy 'Paches make off with a fourteen-year-old kid without doing something about it. But then Pete wasn't a man.

Heck, a *man* would have killed that big son of a bitch Donovan for what he'd done up there in the hay with Ma.

'No, Pete, you'll sit tight and let those red devils roast me alive!

As for Donovan, what could you expect of a big, mean bastard who hunted down other men for money? No blamed bounty hunter was going to risk his life for nothing. Especially for a kid he knew hated his guts.

That left his mother. He didn't want to think of her. If she hadn't been up there in the hay with Donovan he'd have woke her up, and she'd have woke Pete an' none of this would have happened. She hadn't been there when he needed her. She'd cheated on Pete, an' she'd failed him an' ... aw, hell!

He'd still been awake when Delcha launched the dawn attack upon the barn and cabin. That had really scared him. If his folks and Donovan all got killed that would be the end of him, too. But when Delcha and only eight braves returned, he knew the attack had failed.

Despite his resentment, he experienced a certain pride in the defenders. You had to admit that Pete an' Donovan could shoot. An' they sure didn't panic. It was just that fourteen-year-old kid with a big mouth –

113

yeah, a big mouth! – probably didn't count for much.

Maybe they were right.

He was lying propped against the tree, half awake, when Bestinez tossed him over his shoulder and started off through the timber.

Suddenly, he realized what they intended to do to him and fear wound itself into a tight, hard ball inside his stomach and he vomited in great, heaving spasms, the foul mess spilling down Bestinez' stomach and thighs.

The Apache cursed in Spanish and, without breaking stride, slammed his fist against the boy's head.

Along with his consciousness, Tommy Lord's fear went whirling off into space.

Inside the cabin, the three of them waited, sweating out the long hours as the sun climbed above the Rim and gradually warmed up the land.

Not hot yet, but that would come.

By unspoken agreement, they had taken up positions of their own choice:

Donovan in the front room overlooking the meadow...

Simpson covering the corral and the creek from the kitchen...

Peggy Simpson moving restlessly from the bedroom window overlooking the orchard to the kitchen to the front room and then back to the bedroom. The strain was beginning to tell on her. Her mind moved in a continuous circle and, like her feet, always brought her back to the same point.

What would Delcha do to Tommy?

Would Donovan try to rescue the boy as he had promised up there in the mow?

If he failed, what then?

In her thoughts, Pete never occupied any place either inside or outside the circle. Not that she doubted his willingness to go to any lengths to rescue Tommy. She gave him credit for that.

It was simply that this whole situation, from the very beginning, had seemed somehow predestined, with her and Donovan being inexorably drawn toward a point in time which their passion had created.

Returning to the window, she stared out upon the orchard, heavy with fruit, and the garden from which she had already canned enough vegetables for the entire winter, and thought, a little desperately, how fortunate she had been and not known it.

A snug cabin, a swift running creek, plenty of food, a son, a good husband, and a quiet, uneventful life that had been rich in substance despite its isolation. A life and a man, both of which she was just beginning to appreciate when Donovan had ridden in and smashed her snug little world to bits.

Donovan with his amazing understanding and his over-powering maleness, setting her body afire until passion drove all reason from her mind. Yet to blame Donovan would be to ignore her own guilt. After all, Donovan had not lit an innocent virgin. The fire, lighted long ago, had been smoldering for four years. He had only fanned the coals into a hot flame. It was the ease with which he had done so that angered and humiliated her.

Recalling the things Pete had said put her even more on the defensive. Pete had no right to complain. If he had been half a man she would never have gone up there in the mow to begin with. But she'd sworn to kill Donovan unless Pete sent him away. Well, she'd tried and gotten herself raped instead.

Heat rose to her face. Donovan had not pursued her. She had gone to him deliberately, wanting him and knowing that, sensing her passion, he would take her.

And that was the way it had happened.

Now she was trying to hide her guilt

behind the word 'rape'.

For an instant, she felt a surge of intense self-loathing. *When was she going to face up to the fact that she was a whore, pure and simple?*

Then the moment was gone and she was telling herself that if Pete had sent Donovan away like she had begged him to ... dammit, it *had* been rape!

And Pete out there thinking her a whore and feeling sorry for himself!

Well, it was time they had an understanding!

Angrily, she flung open the door.

The moment was ill-timed.

Pete Simpson turned, his face hardening. He had been thinking of the arrogance with which she had flaunted her infidelity. It had been a cruel, senseless act which had served only to further separate them.

Yesterday she had been the center of his life. Now looking at her standing there, a strikingly beautiful woman, it seemed impossible that he should feel nothing for her. Somehow it just did not seem right.

Cut by the thrust of his coldness, Peggy reacted with a quick resentment.

'Don't stand there looking at me like I was a common whore!' she flared. 'Sure, I slept with him! Isn't that what you wanted me to say? All right, I've said it! Now I'll tell you something else. It was good. Do you understand? *It was good!'*

She waited for his reaction, but his face did not change expression. She had the distinct feeling that the only person she was hurting was herself. Yet some compulsive force drove her on.

'And don't think it's over! It's not. Maybe it never will be. I don't know. All I know is that if you'd sent him away – well, it's all your fault!'

Simpson's smile carried no warmth. 'You've always had to have an excuse for this sickness in you, haven't you, Peggy? First Monty, then other men, and now me. Why? It's no one's fault really. You were simply born that way.'

He shook his head. 'I used to think that love and patience would cure you. They won't. You'll keep on until some jealous fool kills you.'

He studied her with an impersonal objectivity. It was still difficult for him to understand his own emotions. His mother's death had affected him the same way. For a long time he had stood beside the coffin studying the wax-like face with its unnatural, painted

118

smile. Then he had turned and walked away, dry-eyed. He could not grieve for something he did not know. And the thing in the box had not been his mother.

Neither was the woman standing before him now his wife Peggy. She was simply ... *nothing*.

'I ought to hate you,' he said. 'But hate is the other side of love. And I don't feel anything for you.'

His coldness cut through Peggy Simpson's anger, hurting her, blunting her attack and crumbling her defenses. She wanted to tell him that he was wrong about her. That his love and patience *had* been slowly but surely destroying the sickness within her. She wanted to remind him of all the strange men who had ridden in and made passes at her while he was away without her ever once betraying him.

She wanted to tell him all these things, but she knew that he would not believe her. It was too late.

Nevertheless, she tried, swallowing her pride, not an easy thing for a proud woman like her to do. Raising her head she stared straight at him.

'I'll not argue with you, Pete. Think what you will. But the truth's the truth. Everything that's happened to us since yesterday afternoon has happened because of this man Donovan.

'*Listen to me!* We're fighting for our lives because of Donovan. I was raped by Donovan. Whatever happens to Tommy will be because of Donovan. If we lose the horse herd, the whole place, you can blame it on Donovan. If we die, it will be Donovan who kills us. We don't even have one another anymore. Why? Donovan! For God's sake, why don't you face up to the facts?'

There was an intensity, a conviction behind her words that disturbed Pete Simpson. Right or wrong, she firmly believed what she said. Could he be the one who was mistaken?

Troubled, he turned away and stared out the window. In the corral, the horse herd moved about quietly. A half dozen chickens scratched industriously in the barnyard. From the orchard he could hear the hammering of a woodpecker.

It was like any other September morning – except for the barn's bullet-splintered walls, the creek bank still wet with Apache blood, the timber where Delcha held Tommy prisoner, the hay mow where Peggy had slept with Donovan, and Peggy herself standing

120

here now boasting of her unfaithfulness.

Those were the *facts*. Why didn't he admit that she was right? If he'd done what she asked, at this very moment he'd be out there working with the herd, with Peggy baking bread in the kitchen and Tommy off somewhere hunting, and all the while that damn jay-bird out there in the tree screeching his head off.

If...

He closed his eyes, trying to shut out the picture. He couldn't go back and change yesterday. He could only try and find the courage to face tomorrow, if there *was* another tomorrow.

Wearily, he turned.

Peggy stood watching him without expression. She had remained simply because she lacked the energy to leave.

Words had never come easy for Pete Simpson. They came even harder now because he wasn't sure himself what he wanted to say.

'Come here, Peggy.'

When she stood beside him, he pointed out the window.

'See that blue jay in the oak? Well, he's a *fact*. But now you tell me why he picked that particular tree on this particular ranch on this particular day to sit and screech his head off and save our lives from an Apache attack.'

Peggy shrugged indifferently. 'He didn't have anything to do with it. It just happened that way. He...' Her face came alive with quick anger.

'Are you trying to tell me that Donovan had nothing to do with all this? That everything has just – *happened?*'

Simpson flushed. 'I'm saying that some things happen because they were meant to happen.'

She tossed her head, her mouth twisting derisively. 'You sound like a fortune teller! Things happen because people make them happen!'

Only hours before, Simpson would have endured her contempt in silence. But those hours had changed him. He stung her with the sharpness of his reply.

'Did Donovan set Chaco on the warpath? Did he make Senator Fleming's daughter take that stagecoach on the day Chaco attacked it? Was he responsible for her rape, her pregnancy or her suicide? Did he talk Fleming into offering a reward for Chaco? Or make Chaco a brave man who chose a bullet instead of a rope? Or give Chaco friends like Delcha to avenge him? Did Donovan make all those things happen? Go ahead – tell me! *Did he?'*

He glared at her, more angry with himself than with her. He was defending a man he should hate and he didn't understand why. Except that Donovan, like them, was a victim of circumstances over which he had no control. In a way, the three of them shared a kind of tragic destiny.

'I still say,' Peggy's voice rose, 'that if it hadn't been for Donovan...'

'You fool!' Simpson felt an almost overpowering urge to hit her. 'Do you think Donovan rode in here just to try and make trouble for us? My God, the Mogollon country was the *last* place he wanted to come to. He spent three weeks trying to break through to Tucson. But not one damn white man in the Territory had the guts to help him. He *had* to come here. Now you blame him for everything that's happened. And me for not turning him over to Delcha.

'Tell me...' Cupping her face in his hands, he forced her to look at him. 'What are *you* to blame for? Getting yourself raped, as you call it?'

A stillness settled over Peggy Simpson's face. 'You don't believe me, do you?'

'No.' Then, defensively. 'If he did, you asked for it. What were you doing up there at two o'clock in the morning anyway?'

'I went up there to kill him.'

'Oh?' Simpson's voice mocked her. 'And why didn't you?'

She had never thought that Pete would be able to hurt her. But he was hurting her now and she didn't know how to stop him. She bit her lips until they clashed with the whiteness of her cheeks.

'I hand-cocked the rifle and fired at his chest. There was no shell in the chamber.'

The mockery faded from Simpson's eyes. 'What happened then?'

'He lunged for the rifle. I fell over backward and he fell on top of me. And then ... well, it just happened.'

'I thought you said things just didn't happen. That people made them happen.'

'I fought as long as there was any point to it.'

Simpson studied her with a painful intensity. It could well have happened the way she claimed. If so, it would help to explain, although not excuse, Donovan.

Alone in a hay mow with a beautiful woman. Furious because the woman had tried to kill him. Wanting to punish her. Hot, sweaty bodies locked together in a struggle over a gun. And then passion rolling over him like a flash flood.

Yes, it could have happened that way. He wished he could believe it had. If he couldn't, then he would eventually have to settle with Donovan.

'You don't believe me, do you?' Peggy said.

'I don't know what to believe,' Simpson told her. 'Maybe if you'd come to me quietly, instead of throwing it in my face the way you did...'

She jerked her head free. 'What you mean is that if I'd crawled to you on my hands and knees it would have saved your pride!' A hard defiance edged her voice. 'I'm not that kind of woman, Pete. I'll not crawl to any man. I was ready to forget the whole affair. But you threw me back at Donovan like I was a worn out whore!'

'What did you expect?' Simpson retorted. 'You sleep with him and then have the gall to come to me and offer to forget what happens. By God, you've got a nerve!'

'Pete, can't you understand?' She addressed him with exaggerated patience. *I'm not ashamed of what happened up there in the mow!* It's the best thing that could have happened to me. For the first time in my life I understand myself. Who I am, what I am, why I am. And why I've done the things I've done. I owe Donovan for that. He opened my eyes and let me out of the swamp.'

'Yet you'd throw him to those 'Paches out there if you got the chance.' Simpson's mouth twisted with disgust. 'You know you're really something!'

Her head lifted defiantly. 'I'm exactly what you said Donovan was. A human being simply trying to save my life and my son's.'

'At the cost of Donovan's?'

'He doesn't care what happens to us! Why doesn't he make a run for it?'

'He wouldn't get a hundred yards.'

She bit her lip, the color rising to her face. 'Then that would be the end of it. Delcha would free Tommy and ride away from here.'

'You're talking like a child!' Simpson snapped. 'Those are 'Paches out there, not white men. Our one hope is Donovan. If he dies, we die. Think of that before you try any more tricks.'

'Oh, shut up! You make me sick!'

They stood there hating one another silently, while long-dormant resentments stirred into life. Hating and loving and not being able to separate the two anymore.

'God!' Peggy stormed into the bedroom, slamming the door behind her.

Simpson poured himself a cup of coffee and sipped it thoughtfully. He had to decide

126

what to do about Donovan and Peggy. Donovan could solve it by getting himself killed; but that would mean the end of all of them. Or he could force Donovan to make a run for it at gun-point. He could, but he knew that he never would. If they survived, Peggy could solve things by going with Donovan.

If none of these things happened, then it would be up to him, Pete Simpson.

How did you go about killing a man you liked? Or throwing out a woman you loved, no matter what she'd done?

Finishing his coffee, he picked up his rifle and went back to the window.

Outside, nothing had changed.

The change was all in him.

He wondered how long it would be before Tommy started to scream. And what he, Pete, would do when it happened.

For Peggy Simpson, it had been a humiliating defeat. For years, she had taken her marriage for granted, treating her husband with an indifferent contempt. Yet all the while hoping that someday he would find the guts to humble her.

Well, it had happened. The Pete Simpson out there in the kitchen was a total stranger. He didn't care whether she lived or died, how many men she slept with, or whether or not she loved him. Certainly he no longer loved her.

It was a frightening thought.

She had all but forgotten those terrible years with Monty Lord. *The champagne-today, water-tomorrow existence.* The paying off of Monty's gambling debts with her body. The insatiable fire in her that nothing could extinguish.

They came back now, those wasted, tormented years, to remind her of the emptiness of her life before she married Pete Simpson.

And before she met Donovan.

Somehow, the two men had merged in her mind to form a third, while still keeping their own identities. And it was this third man who now completely dominated her. It was he whom she both loved and hated, admired and feared, trusted and distrusted. Only he understood her, forgave her and loved her. And up there in the mow it had been he to whom she had given herself completely, without reservation.

With 'him', all things seemed somehow right.

It was only when she had to deal with Pete and Donovan as individuals that she became confused. She had thought them to be exact opposites. The past few hours had proven her wrong. They were basically much alike both in temperament and character.

Except for one inescapable difference.

Donovan overwhelmed her. He was the complete man, capable of turning her into the complete woman. Within less than a day he had made love to her, understood her, gone into the twisted channels of her mind and led her out into the light because he had known she was lost. Without speaking, he shared her emotions, her innermost thoughts, and it all seemed perfectly natural.

With Pete she shared only that which was actually said or done. Most women could be happy with that. She could not be. Contentment was one thing; happiness was another.

Donovan sent her spinning among the stars, played upon her heart strings in a way no man had ever done before, gave her a sense of security and drove her to a frenzy of passion.

Yet she would kill him without hesitation to save her son. Another man she might have shown compassion. But Donovan was above compassion. He could die young and still have experienced more than most men who lived out their years.

This was something Pete could not understand. He measured life in terms of time rather than what one did with that time. But then Pete was not a Donovan and never would be.

Still, he was her husband. Without him she could not survive in this harsh land. If she left him her chances for a third marriage would be very slim. At thirty-two, she was still beautiful, but that beauty would not last forever. And few eligible males would be willing to take on the task of raising a fourteen-year-old boy.

Without money, without friends or any special talent except...

She shivered. Was *that* talent her sole hold upon Donovan? Just what was she to him? Would he take her away from here if she asked him? And if he did would he marry her? Or would he simply use her until he grew tired of her?

She had no answers to any of these questions.

For whereas Donovan knew all about her – her family, Monty, Pete, her other 'loves', even the doll – she knew absolutely nothing about him. Where he came from, who his friends were, what he believed in, if he had ever been anything other than a bounty hunter.

It came to her with a distinct shock that she did not even know his full name. He was simply a desperate man who had ridden into her life and within a few hours ripped it to pieces. One more day and...

Something moved out there in the orchard. She poked the rifle out the window, a new terror seizing her.

She had forgotten Tommy.

It seemed impossible that she could have done this, but she had. She had stood here, with her own son an Apache captive, and let her thoughts center around a future that might never come.

My God, but she was really cracking up!

She waited, her eyes glued to the blackberry patch. And then she saw it. A javelina half hidden among the canes.

For a moment she remained frozen while her mind fought to recover from the shock. Then burying her face in her hands, she fought back the hysteria that was building up inside her.

She was still standing there when she heard Donovan call from the front room.

'Simpson, you'd better get in here!'

'What's the matter?'

Then Donovan replying in a strained voice, 'The boy's out there in the meadow.'

Her knees sagged. *'Oh, my God!'*

She threw open the door and ran through the kitchen, knocking over a chair and bruising her hip but not feeling the pain.

In the front room, Donovan and Pete stood looking out the window with grim faces.

Pete turned quickly, blocking her view.

'Peggy, you'd better go back.'

'Get out of my way!'

Silently, Simpson stepped aside.

Immediately, she wished he hadn't.

Framed in the window, the Mogollon Rim undulated across the horizon like some prehistoric monster. A hundred yards away the meadow drowsed under a warming sun.

At the edge of the meadow, where the grass played out, Tommy Lord lunged frantically at the end of a rawhide *riata* like a panicky colt. His ankles were hobbled. His hands were bound behind his back. A piece of rawhide circled his neck. His chest heaved; his mouth was wide open, gasping. Dark skeins moved aimlessly over his naked, sweating body.

The horror of the scene did not immediately penetrate to Peggy Simpson's distraught mind. Throughout the long hours of the night she had clung to the hope that her son might still be alive. But she had not really believed it. Now just the sight of him out there, lunging against the *riata* like a young animal, filled her with a vast relief.

He was alive. Thank God, he was alive!

Turning to Donovan, she asked in an abnormally calm voice, 'What have they done to him? Why are those black threads all over his body? Why is that rope around his neck? And why is he gasping so hard? They hadn't ought to torment him with that water. He's only a boy.'

It was obvious that she was in shock. She saw but did not comprehend. A merciful respite that would wear off at any moment.

'Go back in the kitchen,' Donovan said gently. 'There's nothing you can do here.'

'What do you mean?' Awareness flooded the brilliant blue eyes. 'That's my son out there!'

'Peggy, please.' Simpson spoke from the other window. 'Do what he says.'

She threw her husband a furious glance. 'You keep out of this! If you hadn't been asleep Tommy wouldn't be out there now!' She focused her attention on Donovan.

'What have they done to him? Tell me! I've every right to know!'

Donovan sensed the hysteria lying just beneath the surface. She would probably crack if he told her the truth. She definitely would if he didn't. Nothing could be gained by lying to her. Sooner or later she was going to have to know the truth.

'All right,' he said. 'To begin with, those are ants crawling all over him. Pretty soon they'll get excited and start stinging. That's a piece of wet rawhide around his neck. When the sun gets hot the rawhide will shrink, slowly. He's gasping because his nostrils are plugged with animal fat. In a little while he won't be able to salivate. His mouth will dry out; his tongue will swell.'

'Go on,' Peggy Simpson whispered through white lips. 'What else?'

'He's had no water for ten or twelve hours. For a fine touch, they've probably made him eat red chilli peppers. That's why he's trying to reach that water. All he's doing is drying himself out that much faster.'

Peggy Simpson shivered. 'Have you finished?' Her voice was barely audible.

'He can't run, hobbled as he is,' Donovan said. 'Even if he could they'd just use the *riata* to haul him back into the grass. They'll do that anyway when they think of something new to...'

'What are you trying to do?' Simpson cried. 'Drive her crazy?'

'And just how long do you think you could have kept the truth from her?' Donovan retorted. 'It's better this way.'

Listening to them with an it's-not-really-happening detachment, Peggy Simpson turned back to the window.

At the moment, young Tommy lifted his head, his mouth opening and closing like a landed fish's, and cried out in a high, boyish voice.

'Ma! Pete! Donovan! Help me! Please help me. *Oh, please, please!*'

'*Aaah!*' With a strangled cry, Peggy Simpson was out the door and running, skirts held high, not hearing the dry snap of rifle fire or the drone of bullets past her head. All her consciousness was centered upon the naked, tormented boy seventy-five yards away.

Donovan caught her in a half dozen strides. She fought him with a wild fury, clawing, scratching, kicking, biting, and all the while screaming, 'Let me go! *Goddamn you! Let ... me ... go!* Oh, you bastard. You big...!'

He laid a hand across her face, knocking her senseless. Slinging her over his shoulder he ran for the cabin. Behind him, Apaches popped up out of the grass, yelling and shooting.

A sharp fire from Simpson drove them back long enough for Donovan to make it inside.

Bullets rapped against the door like heavy knuckles.

In the back room, Donovan laid the woman on the bed. She was still unconscious. A trickle of blood ran from the corner of her mouth.

A pale faced Simpson followed him in. 'Is she all right?'

'Just stunned.'

'Did you have to hit her like that?'

Slowly, Donovan turned, leaning his weight on his rifle. Running, plus the woman's added weight, had reopened his wound. Blood had begun to collect in his boot. He felt weak, dizzy – and angry.

'Would you rather I'd let Delcha have her?'

Simpson was saying something in an apologetic tone but he couldn't understand a word. He tried to focus his eyes upon the rancher, but Simpson's face blurred to a narrow oval far away and then disappeared.

He didn't even know when he went down, his head hitting the floor with a dull thud.

Thoughtfully, Simpson studied the sprawled figure, then looked toward his wife, still unconscious in the bedroom, and, finally, out the window at his stepson lunging mindlessly for the water just out of reach.

Picking up his rifle, he moved toward the door. He knew what he must do, and it must be done quickly.

It was the chilli peppers, chewed and swallowed while a dirty hand covered his mouth and nose, that corroded Tommy Lord's will power.

Until then, he had borne the agony of *cholla* hard-flung against his thighs and buttocks, with a dull stoicism. His initial panic had given way to a sullen determination. If they meant to torture him to death then he would show them that even a fourteen-year-old boy knew how to die.

After they staked him out on the *riata*, he stood there alone, his hands bound behind his back, a wet rawhide noose around his neck and ants crawling over his naked body, and fought against the chilli pepper fire that filled his mouth, seared his throat, and turned his belly into a roaring furnace until he passed water in involuntary indignation.

As the heat of the day began to pull the

moisture from his dehydrated body he sucked in great breaths of air. But instead of cooling his burning tongue, it only parched it. His lips cracked. His tongue swelled to a sausage-like roll that overflowed his mouth. He had now been without water for fifteen hours.

Lying in the grass thirty feet away, Delcha nodded to the stocky Bestinez. The boy was beginning to weaken. It was time to break him.

'Take him the *olla*, Bestinez.'

Slithering through the grass, Bestinez placed the *olla* on the ground, just beyond Tommy Lord's reach. With a smile, the Apache dipped his hand into the *olla* and sluiced the water through his fingers until it gurgled like a tiny brook. Then he snaked his way back through the grass.

The boy stared at the water just out of reach, feeling, in his mind, the coolness of it wetting his cracked lips, flowing down his throat to extinguish the raging fire in his belly.

Cool! Cool as...

He hit the end of the *riata* so hard it snapped him on back, knocking the breath out of him.

It was five minutes before he tried it again.

After that the intervals grew shorter. As his thirst increased his self-control weakened until at last he was lunging against the *riata* like a maddened animal.

Which was exactly what he had become.

Down on his hands and knees, he raised his head and stared at the cabin, so near and yet so hopelessly far away. Suddenly, all the terror and the anguish within him came pouring out of his throat in a shrill, boyish cry.

'Ma! Pete! Donovan! Please help me! *Oh, please, please help me!*'

He saw his mother break from the house and come running toward him with Donovan in hot pursuit ... saw the bounty hunter catch up with her, sling her over his shoulder and run for the cabin.

From the grass behind him, he heard 'Paches yelling and shooting and saw bullets kicking up the dust around Donovan and splinters flying from the cabin's walls like giant yellow straws.

Now, at last, he understood why he was being tortured. Like a staked-out yearling, he was the bait to draw Donovan into the open. He was going to die here, slowly, in full view of the cabin so they could all hear him screaming.

'Donovan!' he yelled. 'Do you hear me? You big, mean son of a bitch, do something! *Please!*'

Screaming and crying, he raced in a thirty foot circle, obsessed by a frantic yearning for release from his agony.

And then the ants began to sting.

He stopped crying.

Now he just screamed.

Consciousness returned to Donovan with no sense of interrupted action. One moment he was listening to Pete Simpson. The next he was lying on the floor watching the rancher's booted feet move toward the door.

Pushing to his knees, he grabbed his rifle. 'Try it, Simpson, and I'll lame you for life.'

The rancher whirled, his face dark with anger. 'You think I'm going to watch him tortured to death?'

'Getting yourself killed won't help him.'

'You went out there after Peggy.'

It was a challenge, an accusation, a defense and a question all rolled into six words.

Donovan put his knees against a chair and sat down heavily. 'That was different,' he said. 'Delcha thought I was going for the boy. By the time he realized his mistake, I hoped to have her back inside. That's the way it worked out.'

The line of Simpson's jaw hardened. 'You'd have gone right into the middle of them after her if you'd had to. Are you in love with her?'

It was a loaded question and Donovan ignored it. Simpson was pushing him hard. Yet it was the boy, not the woman, who was the rancher's real concern. Reason told Simpson he could not save his stepson; emotion told him he must try. And in be-tween logic and emotion a dark thought was forming.

Swap Donovan for the boy. It's the only way.

Remembering Victorio back in Tucson, Donovan wondered whether, in Simpson's position, he would have reacted any differently. The thought tempered his tone when he answered.

'The boy's in no immediate danger,' he said. 'If he dies, Delcha loses his only chance to take me alive. He knows that.'

'Tommy doesn't know it,' Simpson retorted. 'Even if he did, it wouldn't help him out there now, screaming his head off.'

'He's scared as much as anything.'

'*Scared!*' Simpson exploded. 'My God, what are you, some kind of monster? That kid's going through hell!'

'Maybe it will make a man out of him.' A

new, harsh note deepened Donovan's voice. 'Indian boys are trained to endure torture.'

'He's no damned 'Pache!' Simpson flared. 'He's a fourteen-year-old kid who can't understand what happening to him or why.'

Silently, Donovan unpinned his soaked trouser leg. He wiggled his foot and felt blood squishing up between his toes.

'I need some more bandages.'

Simpson did not move. 'I want to know about the boy.'

'We're staying in here until Delcha realizes I'm not going to take the bait.'

'You mean you're just going to sit here and...' Simpson's face went slack with disbelief. 'Why, Goddamn you!'

Sitting there, Donovan was struck by the incongruity of the situation. He was quietly and painlessly bleeding to death because he could not make Pete Simpson realize that sometimes it was necessary to be cruel in order to be kind.

'I'll not let him die,' he said tonelessly.

He pushed to his feet and limped into the bedroom.

Peggy Simpson stirred but did not open her eyes as he tore off a wide strip of her petticoat. Satisfied she was all right, he returned to the kitchen and applied a pressure bandage to his leg.

Blood dripped steadily to the floor as he worked.

In the front room, Pete Simpson paced back and forth, keeping away from the window and trying to shut out the sound of Tommy's screaming, hoarser and much weaker now.

Damn you, Donovan, why don't you give yourself up?

He could not help thinking it; he could even reluctantly wish for it to happen. But he could not ask the big man to do it. Donovan had already risked his life three times for the Simpson family. There was a limit to how much you could ask of a man.

Ask? They had not had to ask. Donovan had just done it, then shrugged it off as nothing.

That was the amazing thing about the man. He sensed situations, sized them up, and then dealt with them without fanfare. If his methods were sometimes harsh they were, nonetheless, effective.

He was like no other man Pete Simpson had ever known. Difficult to understand and even more difficult to maintain a fixed attitude toward. As the situation changed, so also did Pete Simpson's emotions. One moment he liked the bounty hunter. The next he wanted to kill him.

That was the woman's fault. It was she who had put them at one another's throats.

It was the 'woman' now, and the knowledge deeply disturbed Simpson. His whole life seemed to be fragmenting, flying off into a hundred directions while he stood helplessly by, watching it happen.

He wondered if perhaps it must not also seem that way to the woman. And, yes, to Donovan.

But it was Tommy who was least prepared to understand. The boy's whole life had been warped by misunderstanding. About his father, law and justice, strength and weakness, and, most of all, about himself. A fourteen-year-old kid, caught up in a riptide of uncertainty and rejection, struggling to find acceptance in a world of grown-ups who had forgotten what it was like to be fourteen and scared. Grown-ups who stood around arguing while a boy was being put to the torture.

Suddenly, he became aware of the silence. He stood listening, conscious of the rapid beat of his heart.

Something was wrong.

And then it came to him.

Tommy had stopped screaming.

He ran to the window.

Overhead, a buzzard circled lazily against a cloudless sky. A faint breeze stirred the tall grass of the empty meadow.

Tommy Lord was gone.

She was in the yard, struggling to break away from Donovan, with Apaches yelling and bullets humming around her and Tommy out there screaming horribly and...

Pain. Heavy, pounding pain that beat rhythmically inside her head, pulverizing her thoughts.

She lay perfectly still, her eyes shut tight against the light, letting her fingers trace out and identify the familiar pattern of the counterpane.

Slowly she turned her head, setting her teeth to the pain, and opened her eyes. Sunlight slanted in through the window and splashed across her face. She waited, listening for someone, something to break the unnatural silence. Where were Pete and Donovan? What had happened out there in the yard after Donovan had hit her? Had both men been killed trying to save her? No, she would be dead, too.

Tommy!

A sudden spasm of nausea rolled her over, head hanging over the side of the bed. She heaved violently, bringing up a gush of watery bile.

After a while, she sat on the edge of the bed, weak and dizzy but her head not hurting quite so bad now. Her mouth felt dry, sour tasting. She wondered if she could make it to the pump in the kitchen for a drink.

She was still debating the matter when she heard a rush of footsteps across the front room. And then Pete crying out, *'My God!'* The words were low and drawn out, as though hating to be said. *'Tommy's gone!'*

A roaring wind tore through her mind shredding all reason. Then it was gone, leaving behind a strange calm.

It was over, done with. Tommy was dead. He had died out there alone while she had lain unconscious, unable to help or even to pray for him.

Donovan had let him die.

Her mind snapped on the thought like a bear trap, refusing to let go.

She slid her legs over the edge of the bed and stood up. She felt suddenly very strong and clear-headed.

Moving quietly, she went into the kitchen. From the front room, she could hear the low murmur of voices but she was not longer interested. She knew all she needed to know. Now but one thought filled her mind.

To the center of the room ... the kitchen table ... the foot-long butcher knife, razor sharp...

Her hand closed around the wooden haft. Now the knife became a part of her, an extension of her arm, of the hate in her heart.

Quietly she slipped into the front room.

Pete stood at the window, staring outside.

Donovan had his back to her, his huge shoulders all but blocking her view.

She came up soundlessly behind him, so close that she could smell the maleness of him in the heat of the room.

The knife felt heavy, solid in her hand, the wooden haft slippery with perspiration.

She drove the point at a spot just under Donovan's left shoulder.

At that instant, Simpson turned, saw her, and yelled, *'Look out!'*

Had the big man whirled he would have taken the blade in his chest. Instead, he dropped to his knees and Peggy Simpson, lunging, fell over him. Before she could recover, Donovan wrenched the knife from her hand.

She went at him silently then, savagely, with fists, feet, teeth, and finally, with raking fingernails. When the strength was gone from her and she could no longer strike out, she spat in his face and screamed, 'You beast! Why did you let him die? Why didn't you give yourself up? *Why?*'

Pulling her up with him, Donovan shook her until she slumped against him from complete exhaustion. The blood-thirsty bitch would never be satisfied until she killed him.

'My God, woman!' he said. 'What's the matter with you? Your son is alive. Do you understand? *Tommy is alive!*'

'Liar!' She went at him again, drawing on some inner reserve. 'I heard what Pete said. He's gone!'

Pete Simpson wrenched her away, pinning her arms to her sides. 'Get hold of yourself! They've just taken him back into the timber. That's all.'

She stopped fighting. 'Are you sure?'

'I'm sure.'

Impulsively, she twisted in his arms, laying her head against his chest and found a strange comfort in the steady beat of his heart.

Then the moment was gone. Thrusting

him away, she said, 'They'll torture him again.'

Simpson just looked at her.

She whirled on Donovan. 'Well, what do you intend to do?'

Back-sleeving his bloody face, Donovan resisted the urge to hit her. She was like no other woman he had ever known. A mass of contradictions constantly warring against one another. Loving one moment, hating the next, and ready to murder whenever the mood struck her.

Simpson could have her and welcome.

'Well, answer me! What are you going to do?'

'I'm going to hog-tie you to the bed if you don't calm down,' Donovan snapped. 'I'm getting tired of you trying to kill me.'

'I hate you!'

'Be careful that hate doesn't kill us all.'

'Please, Donovan, I can't take anymore.'

Sensing her distress, Donovan relented. 'All right, then listen to me. Until I surrender, Delcha has no choice but to keep the boy alive. That gives us time to figure out some way to rescue him.'

'You mean you'll let them torture Tommy again?'

'No more than he can stand.'

'My God,' Peggy cried passionately, 'hasn't he suffered enough already?'

Donovan's face took on a grim cast. 'He'll just have to sweat it out.'

'I'd rather you shot him and put him out of his misery!'

'If I can't save him I will.'

There was no softening of the woman's features. 'You can save him anytime. All you've got to do is give yourself up. Then Delcha will free Tommy and ride away and leave us alone.'

'Either you're a fool,' Donovan said, 'or you just don't understand Apaches.'

'She believes what she wants to believe,' Pete Simpson turned to his wife. 'Half an hour ago I was thinking the same way. Don't you realize that you could give Delcha Donovan's head on a pole and it wouldn't save Tom or us. 'Paches kill just for the fun of it. Our only chance is to stick together. The three of us.'

Peggy Simpson's face turned livid with rage. 'You weak-kneed, spineless excuse for a man! Don't you stand there and tell me—'

The back of Simpson's hand caught her full on the mouth, flattening her lips against her teeth. She reeled away, her eyes child-wide with disbelief.

'You've had that coming for a long time,' Simpson said calmly.

He looked at her, glaring at him in open-mouthed outrage; and, for the first time, he saw her as a woman, not as an unattainable ideal. It was a strange sensation, a feeling of release from a life-long conviction that woman was either perfect or a whore. Too late, he realized that no woman was perfect and that there was a little of the whore in all of them.

Suddenly he wanted to take her in his arms and tell her that he understood every-thing, even her affair with Donovan. But he knew that he couldn't because he under-stood nothing.

That had been his trouble from the begin-ning. He had never understood her. He had simply tried to accept her at face value, without any idea of what she was like inside.

He didn't know her at all.

'Peggy.'

She turned. Blood trickled from the corner of her mouth. She wiped it away with the back of her hand.

'It doesn't matter,' she said. 'You never had any use for whores anyway.'

Simpson finger-combed his hair with a weary gesture. 'Peggy, will you listen to me for a...'

He was talking to an empty doorway.

As he moved to follow her, Donovan blocked his way. 'Why don't you leave her alone for a while. She's all mixed up.'

'She's been mixed up ever since you rode in,' Simpson retorted.

'Well, you're not helping her any, treating her like a whore.'

'Have you got a better name for her?'

'She's a man's woman,' Donovan replied coldly. 'She needs to be dominated. It makes her feel secure. For a few hours I filled that need. Now it's over, done with.'

'It will never be over!' In sudden anguish, Simpson slammed his fist against the wall. 'Why did she have to turn to you?'

Lowering himself into a chair, Donovan stretched his wounded leg out in front of him. The bleeding had stopped but a painful stiffness had begun to set in. He shifted to a more comfortable position.

'She has no respect or confidence in you,' he said. 'From her way of thinking, you've never taken a stand for or against anything in your life.'

The rancher's mouth took on a stubborn set. 'A man has his hands full running his own life without meddling in other people's.'

Donovan shook his head in perplexity. 'I don't understand you, Simpson. You stay out of trouble all of your life. Then, suddenly, you risk everything you have – your ranch, your marriage, even the lives of your family – for a man you never saw until yesterday. Why?'

Simpson spun angrily, his face dark with frustration. 'Hell, it's all in black and white. I've got no choice.'

'You've always had a choice.'

'Of turning you over to Delcha? I wouldn't do that to any man.'

'Most people would say I had it coming to me.'

'You'll get what you deserve.'

Hooking his arms around his chair back, Donovan stared thoughtfully at the rancher. 'Do you think killing me would change things? She'd still have the same hunger; and there would always be a man to light her.'

'The way you did?'

With a honey slow motion, Donovan unhooked his arms. Then he said quietly, 'I didn't have to light her, Simpson.'

'Shut your mouth!'

'You're the one who keeps calling her a

whore,' said Donovan. 'Not me.'

'I've got the right.' Then, thickly: 'I ought to kill you both!'

Imperceptibly, Donovan's face took on a dangerous expression. It was clear that Simpson meant to force a fight sooner or later. And once a man like that made up his mind, he simply closed his ears and shut you out. There was nothing you could do then save stay alert.

'You know what's eating you?' he said. 'She's too much woman for you. You don't understand her, and you can't handle her. What you need is a simple-minded, barefoot wench who will...'

Simpson hit him, a short, hard right that rocked him back in his chair, not hurting much, but it was something no man had ever done before. A dark, terrible force stirred deep within him and began to slowly uncoil in his brain.

He closed his eyes, breathed deeply, and waited until the thing in his brain stilled. Then he said in a low, flat voice, 'There's a boy out there in real trouble. If he wasn't, I'd kill you. The next time I *will* kill you.'

Rubbing his knuckles, Simpson fought to bring his temper under control. 'Or I'll kill you.'

154

Donovan picked up his rifle and moved toward the kitchen.

'Then we understand one another.'

'One more thing.'

Donovan turned, frowning.

'Stay away from her.'

'Like I said...' Donovan's tone was easy. 'She came to me. If she wants to do it again that's her business. Now I'm going to the barn. If they bring the boy out again don't do anything foolish. Delcha's hoping that one of us will crack up.'

'What do you intend to do?'

'Work things out my own way.'

In the kitchen, he stuffed a loaf of bread and a chunk of beef into a flour sack. Then replenishing his ammunition, he started out the back way.

As he passed the bedroom, Peggy Simpson turned away from the window and called, 'Donovan?'

'Yes?'

'Can you save Tommy?'

'Maybe,' Donovan said. 'If you and Pete don't mess things up again.'

'I'm sorry.' Her manner was suddenly contrite. 'I just don't seem to be able to stand up to things, do I?'

'It's not just you. It's beginning to tell on

us all.'

She came toward him, the blue of her eyes darkening until the pupils were almost black. The tip of her tongue moved with a lazy sensuality around her parted lips.

'Take me back to the barn with you, Donovan.'

She was incredible, he thought. Given the chance, she would surrender him to Delcha to torture to death, use him to strike back at her husband, sacrifice him to save her son, sleep with him or try to kill him, as the mood and the situation dictated. Yet an intense, unsatisfied need bound her to him, forcing these capitulations.

'No,' he said firmly.

She moved in until her high rising breasts flattened against his chest. 'Pete's beginning to crack up. I'm afraid of him.'

'I wouldn't worry about it,' Donovan said. 'You've never met a man you couldn't handle.'

Anger blazed briefly in her eyes. Then she said in a voice that was quietly bitter, 'Except you!'

Stepping back, she made no protest as Donovan went outside.

For a moment Donovan flattened himself

against the cabin wall, watching the timber across the creek. Then, bent low, he raced for the shelter of the big oak. There he commanded a view of the corral, the barn, and the creek. He put down the grub sack, levered a shell into the Winchester, and waited.

An oppressive silence had settled over the land. Off to the northwest, ominous black clouds boiled up over the horizon and muted thunder rolled along the Mogollon Rim. Dimmed by the early afternoon sun, sheet lightning flickered pale yellow across the sky. The air grew humid, making it hard to breathe.

Donovan frowned. Perhaps he should go back to the cabin. He knew the fury of these mountain storms and of the flash floods which swept down from higher up, turning creeks into raging torrents that destroyed everything in their path – men, animals, ranches.

Even as he crouched there, hesitant, great greenish-tinged clouds rushed across the sky, blotting out the sun. Although it was not yet two o'clock an eerie dusk settled over the land giving trees a waxy cast and the soil a soft reddish-pink tinge.

In the corral, the horse herd milled about,

nervously testing the air, while blue jays, sparrows, woodpeckers and crows dipped and soared in raucous confusion.

A freshening wind blew damply against Donovan's face, building quickly to short, hard gusts. A few big rain drops bounced off the oak leaves and pocked the dusty yard.

Suddenly, for a long way off, Donovan heard it coming, roaring through the Ponderosas, ripping the saddle-high oak brush and manzanita and filling the air with a smothering torrent of rain.

Too late now to make it back to the cabin.

He broke cover and ran for the barn with the wind-driven rain sweeping through the orchard behind him, lashing the trees and scattering fruit everywhere, then booming on through the garden, leaving corn flattened and vegetables pounded into the quick-mud.

He barely made it, with just enough time to yank the door shut and drop the cross bar in place before the storm struck.

A solid sheet of water hit the barn, hammering the roof and walls like hail. Then the eighty-mile-an-hour wind slammed against the heavy logs knocking out loose chinking and blowing small rivulets of water inside.

In her stall, the brood mare neighed in terror, splintering the side boards with lashing hoofs.

Stumbling around in the darkness, it seemed to Donovan that the whole world had become a roaring chaos of wind and water, thunder and lightning.

Carefully he worked his way to the ladder. He had a foot on the bottom rung when the colt, thrown sometime during the night, ran headlong into him.

He dropped the grub sack and grabbed the panic-stricken little creature. In her terror, he knew that the mare might accidentally kick it to death. And if he put it outside it would drown or suffocate within minutes.

He laid down his rifle, hoisted the colt under one arm, and side-stepped his way up the ladder.

In the weird light of the mow, he put the colt in a 'corral' of hay bales and threw a piece of canvas over the top to shut out the lightning.

Wind and a heavy spray of rain were whistling in through the gun ports. Quickly Donovan closed and secured them.

The mow window, on the lee side, he left open; and from there he looked out upon a violent, unreal world. Creek, timber, and horizon were gone, swallowed up by a roaring, screaming, wind-torn darkness constantly shredded by lightning and barraged by cannonading thunder.

Once, he thought he heard the mare kicking against the sides of her stall but it could have been debris hurled against the barn.

Suddenly he remembered his rifle and the grub sack. He went back down into the smothering darkness, retrieved his gear and returned to the mow.

There, close under the roof, he listened to the wind rippling at the cedar shakes and the drum-like roll of the rain and the ear-splitting crack as lightning struck a tree across the creek.

He thought of the boy Tommy out there in all that fury and wondered if the kid's mind and body could absorb the savage punishment.

Even the Apaches would be taking a beating. With wind toppling trees and lightning riving others, the timber provided no protection. Like the rest of the valley, it was flatland with no hills in the lee of which men could find shelter, nor caves in which to build a fire against the numbing cold which had replaced the mid-day heat.

Nor could Delcha hope for any quick relief. These storms, although abating in intensity, sometimes lasted for several days.

With game scarce, the days cold and wet and the nights even worse, and with the White Eyes snug and warm in their cabin and barn, Apache morale was bound to...

The barn! Suppose they hadn't seen him out there under the oak? Suppose they thought he was still in the cabin with the others?

The barn would be the first place they would think of to take shelter.

He went back to the window and stared down into the blackness directly below. Lightning flamed against the sky, throwing the side of the barn into brilliant 'day-lightness' – and he saw them.

Five Apaches crouched beneath the window, staring up at him open-mouthed, with Tommy Lord, still naked, draped across one buck's shoulder.

Then the light was gone.

Whipping up his rifle, Donovan waited for the next flash. When it came, the spot beneath the window was empty.

They must have tried the barn door first and, finding it locked, had hoped to gain entrance through the mow window. Now they had nowhere else to go. Neither the toolhouse nor the woodshed would shelter them; and an attack against the cabin in this weather would be suicidal.

Opening a gun port, Donovan fired three shots, deliberately high, toward the outbuildings. They would keep Delcha moving and alert Pete Simpson.

For a while, at least, the action was over.

Laying aside his rifle, Donovan sat down on the hay and helped himself from the grub sack. He ate slowly, his mind concerned more with the digestion of facts than of food.

The sight of Tommy Lord naked out in the cold, slashing rain had upset him. It meant a radical change of plans. He would have to abandon his decision to convince Delcha that he would never surrender to save Tommy Lord.

At first, he had tried to think of Tommy as a man, tormented by fire in his belly, slowly strangling to death from a wet rawhide noose around his throat, half crazed by acid-skeins of ants winding around his naked body, and maddened by thirst and the sight of the *olla* of water only inches out of reach.

A *man*, he told himself, should be able to stand those things for quite a while if he had to. And you *expected* him to if other lives were at stake.

So he had reluctantly forced himself to

think *man,* not boy; and it had worked until Tommy had suddenly raised his head and cried out in a shrill, boyish voice, 'Ma! Pete! Donovan! Help me! *Please help me!'*

Then it was no longer a man out there, but a scared fourteen-year-old kid who'd never even had his first sweetheart or store-bought suit or known any kind of real pain that would prepare him for the unending agony.

After Peggy Simpson's near-fatal attempt to rescue her son, Donovan had realized that he would probably have to abandon his plan.

Now with the lightning-etched picture of the boy's naked body being pounded by chilling rain fresh in his mind, he knew that he could not go through with it.

He would have to find another way.

As soon as the storm let up he would go after Tommy Lord. He would not come back without him.

Meanwhile, he could do nothing but sweat out the long hours. He was used to that. But now there was a restlessness within him that would not let him relax.

He thought of Peggy Simpson and of the violence of their passion in the mow the night before. If he had re-lit the fire in her, she had done more than that to him.

She had penetrated the barrier which, all his life, he had kept between himself and decent women. He wanted not merely her body; he wanted her as a woman with whom he could share his future and who would bear him a son. Yet these things were not for him and he knew it.

Even the thought that she might become pregnant as a result of those moments in the hay filled him with a dark foreboding.

It was the nightmare relived, this time with himself in his father's role and Peggy Simpson that of his mother. The fact that his parents had been married and that he had been conceived in love rather than in violent passion did not alter the nightmare. It had been the child who had...

A faint whinny from the colt cut through his thoughts. He threw back the canvas and with a gentle hand stroked the sweat-soaked little body until the trembling stopped and a velvety nose nuzzled him in gratitude. Then he rose and limped to the window.

For a long time, he stood staring out into the storm, listening to the wind rise to a higher and higher pitch until it mingled with and then became the wind his father must have heard banging the shutters of the brownstone town house when it had happened.

It had been on just such a night, with high winds and raging seas sending the great clipper ships racing for the shelter of Boston harbor, that Donovan had been born, literally ripping his way into the world while his mother screamed out her life on the blood-soaked fourposter bed.

The day after his wife's funeral, Charles had departed Boston and did not return for a full year. When he did, he quietly took up where he had left off, offering no explanation as to his whereabouts during that period.

Within a month, he closed the town house, and thereafter divided his time between his club and his country estate, *Golden Dunes*.

Although only thirty years old and much sought after by Back Bay Boston debutantes, he never remarried. He remained a courteous, magnificent figure of a man, but the inner fire had burned out of him.

During the years following her death, his love for his wife grew rather than faded. But it never took unto itself that part of her which had so murderously killed that it might live.

How could a man love a child who, for him, did not exist?

According to Dr Jerimah Stone, who had delivered the child, and Mistress Millicent Davies, the boy's governess, that was precisely the father's attitude toward his offspring.

He had no son.

True, there was a child on the estate, but he never saw it. Attended by a governess, a cook-housekeeper and a valet groom companion, the boy occupied a comfortable cottage a quarter of a mile from the main house.

Although visitors, from time to time, observed the child in the company of its governess, they never asked questions of the master of *Golden Dunes*.

Nor did he ever speak of the boy. To him, it was not flesh of his flesh, but an alien force that had invaded his wife's body and killed her. He provided for its welfare because it was his Christian duty, and because the law required it. Had it died he would not have grieved, for often in his heart he wished it dead.

He lived another twenty years, amassed a huge fortune in banking and shipping enterprises, and died without ever acknowledging the existence of his son.

Neither did that son, who had left *Golden Dunes* in 1859 to attend Havard College and dropped out to join the Union Army after the firing on Fort Sumter, turn up to claim his rights.

Years later, Dr Jerimah Stone sought to explain the tragedy to a group of friends gathered in his study for after-dinner brandy and cigars.

'Although associates considered him cold and aloof, Charles was by nature a kind man, utterly devoted to his wife. To lose her after only two years of marriage...' The doctor shook his head. 'Charles just couldn't reconcile himself to her death. Or accept the fact that the child could not be held responsible. Better to blame it on me if blame had to be attached to anyone.'

He sipped moodily on his brandy. Then reading the question in his guests' eyes, he continued.

'Had Janice had a difficult pregnancy? No, that was what made the thing so terrible. Aside from morning sickness the first couple of months, she was in excellent health.

'Of course, I knew the child would be large. After all, Charles was a big man, six feet four or five, I'd say, and weighing close to two hundred and forty pounds. And Janice herself was a tall, well-formed woman with a fine pelvis. The ideal child-bearing type. There was no reason to expect any complication.'

The memory of that night still haunted Jerimah Stone. He took a handkerchief from his pocket and daubed at his perspiring face.

'Janice wanted the child born at home and I consented. That was a mistake. Perhaps if she'd been in a hospital I could have done a Cesarian. No, it wouldn't have made any difference. It all happened too quickly.'

He took a deep breath, then continued in a voice that was not quite steady.

'My God, nothing about that birth was normal! Her water broke too soon. Once labor started, the child ignored contractions. It actually fought its way out, as though it couldn't wait to get on with the business of living. Before I knew it one arm and half the head was out. Then it stuck.

'That was when Janice started to scream; and from then until she died she never stopped screaming. My God, it was horrible! My trying to position the child and feeling the stubborn thrust of the head against my hand, and Janice screaming, and the blood making my hands so slippery I couldn't...'

He gulped down the rest of his brandy, then looked at his silent guests wanting to transfer some of the horror of those moments from his mind to theirs and thus relieve himself of his guilt.

'If it had been just the head,' he continued more calmly, 'she might have lived. I was able to free it. But the *entire* child – do any of you have the faintest idea of what an *eighteen pound* baby looks like coming out of the birth canal pulling the womb with it, while its mother screams her life away?

'That is why Charles hated his son. In those first moments of madness, he would have killed it had the nurse not fled from the room with it.

'And that, gentlemen, is also why I sometimes hate myself.'

'Nonsense, Jerimah,' Lucius Alread, a long time friend, protested. 'You did everything you could.'

'At the time perhaps,' Stone replied. 'But that wasn't what I meant.'

'I don't understand.'

Jerimah Stone concentrated upon his long, spatulate fingers. 'You might say I failed the boy just as I failed his mother. I never explained to him why his father hated him. Or even that Charles was his father, although he eventually guessed the truth. In fact, I did nothing to help him to understand his ostracism or to bear his loneliness.'

Lucius Alread's face mirrored his astonishment. 'Why would you do a thing like that?'

'Because I was a damned coward,' Jerimah Stone said in a dull voice. 'Now if you gentlemen will excuse me, I think I've talked enough for one night.'

After they had gone, he refilled his glass, lighted up a fresh cigar, and sat staring at the dying flames on the hearth.

If he or Millicent Davies had told Donovan the truth when the boy first asked them...

But neither of them had had the courage. Charles had been a man of great influence in Boston. To have opposed him, especially under the circumstances, would have been extremely unwise.

Millicent Davies had not only feared the loss of her position, she was actually afraid of Charles during those last few years. Perhaps they all were. For beneath the courteous, well-bred exterior, there had been a touch of madness in Charles after his wife's death. Dormant, yes, but not needing much to set it off.

As a brilliant young physician with a promising future, Jerimah Stone had not wished to compromise that future. He had, therefore, become a party to Charles' cruelty on the day the banker issued instructions to the special staff assigned to care for the boy.

'I shall be very explicit,' Charles said. 'To begin with, the child has no name. Do you understand. *No name.* He is to be addressed as *child, Young Master,* and *Young Sir,* in that order, as he grows older.

'When he asks his name, you are to say you do not know. When he asks who his father is, you are to say that he has no father. When he asks who I am, you will remain silent. Failure to do so will result in immediate dismissal. Moreover, I shall see to it that you never again secure employment in Boston. That is all.'

He had put his back to them and said coldly to Jerimah Stone, 'You will observe the privileged relationship in this matter, sir. Unethical conduct is, I believe, treated very harshly in the medical profession. Good day, Doctor.'

Charles had known they were weak, all of

them. That was why he had chosen them. As such, they had served him well, maintaining a tight-lipped silence over the years.

In this atmosphere, the boy had grown up.

Jerimah Stone stared moodily into the dying embers, finding little comfort in the warmth of the brandy to which he resorted more and more frequently for peace of mind.

Just when Donovan realized that Charles was his father he was never able to recall. But it could not have been prior to his eighth birthday because until then he had never seen the master of *Golden Dunes*.

'Cookie' had baked him a huge chocolate cake decorated with candles and *Happy Birthday, Young Master,* in white frosting, and had cried because he had no name for her to put on it. Frank Miller, the valet-groom, a little drunk on too much celebrating, had said indignantly:

'It's not right that the lad should have no name, *some* kind of name, and he's beginning to realize it. Every day it's the same question. "Father, why don't I have a name?" And when I tell him I'm not his father, he asks who his father is, and I tell him, "Lad, you have no father," and the lie hurts my tongue.

'But is he satisfied with that? No, I tell you he is a smart one, he is. He looks at me and says, "Sir, every boy has to have a father. Is my father dead?"' Miller shook his head in helpless anger.

'Now what can I tell him? You heard the Master. "Silence," he said. And so I don't even tell him, "Yes, lad, your father is dead," and at least let him believe he had a father. No, I keep my mouth shut, just like the rest of you. A fine lot we are, gaolers paid to torment a little boy by keeping from him his birthright!'

He sat down at the table opposite the governess. 'And what do you tell him, Mistress Davies, when he calls you Mother and asks you why he hasn't a name and who his father is? Do *you* tell him the kind lie – that, yes, you are his mother and that his father is dead?

'No, Mistress Davies, you do the same as I do. You tell him just enough to hurt him. That you are not his mother, that he has no father, not even a name; and then you walk away and leave him standing there, blinking his eyes.'

Millicent Davies lifted her head and tried to stare him down, but his eyes met hers with a knowing cynicism and after a moment she flushed and turned away.

'What would you have me do, Mister Miller? I'm thirty years old, a not very attractive spinster with no dowry and, hence, virtually no prospect of marriage. If I angered Mister Charles I would never secure another position as governess in all New England.'

She turned a white, strained face toward him. 'You think me so heartless that I don't cry every time he asks me those questions? Say what you will, weak and selfish as I am, I love him. We all do. So if we have to hurt him to stay with him, then we'll hurt him. For without us he'd have no love at all.'

The three of them sat there with the late October sun streaming through the kitchen windows, and an understanding was born between them that was to endure for eight long, very difficult years.

At last Miller, a kind, sensitive man with some small knowledge of books and a great deal more of life, said quietly, 'Mistress Davies, I am not often given to apology. But I have misjudged you and for that I do humbly apologize. Seeing Hannah sitting here crying, and that big fine cake with no name on it...'

He looked at the cake, at the eight candles

and the *Happy Birthday, Young Master* and his mouth took on a stubborn set.

'It's not right. Everyone should have a name. And especially little boys. Hannah...' he smiled at the cook and somehow it changed his whole face, 'can you mix up another batch of that frosting?'

'Why, yes, I suppose so,' Hannah said. 'But...' she threw a quick glance of half fear, half delight at the governess, 'do you suppose we dare, Mistress Davies?'

'I think it would be the nicest birthday present any small boy ever had,' Millicent Davies replied. 'But what shall it be?'

'I've had it in mind for a long time,' Miller said. 'And I think it fits him.'

'Well, then, tell us, sir.'

'Donovan.'

A horrified expression darkened Millicent Davies' face. 'Surely you can't be serious! Naming a little boy after a...'

'A horse?' Miller said calmly. 'And why not? The stallion's a thoroughbred. Big, strong, intelligent, and all heart. He'll never be tamed. The master knows that. It's why the stallion's never known the touch of steel or leather. He'd kill himself fighting. He should have been born free.'

'But to name the boy...!'

175

'That little boy and that stallion have a lot more in common that most fathers and sons. Anything you say about the one will fit the other. Well, ladies, what say you?'

'Yes!' Hannah exclaimed. 'I think it's a fine name!'

'And you, Mistress Davies?'

'You'll have to hurry, Hannah.' She pushed back her chair and rose. 'I told him three o'clock and it's a quarter of three now.'

'Why don't you go get him?' Hannah said. 'By the time he's washed his face and hands, I'll have it ready.'

The boy was standing on the lawn facing the westering sun. He was larger than the average boy his age but well-proportioned. His face, when he turned to Millicent Davies, was grave, the wide spaced eyes marked by a disturbing intensity.

'Miss Millie,' he said, pointing to the main house, 'who is the tall man walking over there? Is he a giant, like in the stories you read to me? Is he?'

Quickly Millicent Davies took him by the hand and hurried him toward the cottage. 'Never you mind who he is,' she said. 'We're going to be late for your party unless you can wash up real fast. Can you do that?'

'Yes, Miss Millie,' he said, and ran on

ahead of her.

She hesitated, then risked a furtive glance toward the main house.

The master of *Golden Dunes* stood motionless, tall and massive against the skyline, staring toward her.

She turned and fled to the cottage, wondering if he, too, remembered that this was his son's birthday.

It was the first time the boy had ever seen his father, and it gave Millicent Davies a strange comfort that she had kept the truth from him.

And so it was that on October 18, 1852, Mistress Millicent Davies, Mrs Hannah Ellers, and Frank Miller, without the knowledge or consent of the 'Master', placed before an eight-year-old boy a huge cake with brightly burning candles and decorated with the words *Happy Birthday, Master Donovan* in white frosting.

'Do you like it, lad?' Frank Miller asked.

'Oh, yes, sir!' The boy smiled and lifted quiet eyes to his governess. 'What does it say, Miss Millie?'

'Why, it says...' Millicent Davies caught her breath, 'it says *Happy Birthday, Donovan!*'

Then spontaneously spinster, cook, and valet-groom broke into *'Happy birthday, dear*

Donovan, Happy birthday to you!'

He sat there, eight years old, looking at the huge cake with its bright, flickering candles and his name in white frosting on top while the tears rolled down his face.

It was the only time they ever saw him cry.

Children were not permitted at *Golden Dunes*.

Weekend guests were always courteously informed well in advance that there were not the proper 'facilities' for the care and entertainment of the younger set. Thus Charles insured himself the personal privacy which he desired while, at the same time, keeping the boy away from curious friends.

Although all Boston knew of the tragic death of his young wife years before, very few were acquainted with the exact events of that terrible night. It was against these few, however, that Charles so carefully protected himself. He wanted no carelessly dropped word to betray the child's identity.

It was not until the summer of 1860, when Donovan was sixteen, that the boy met a girl his own age.

He was walking along the four-foot-high fence separating *Golden Dunes* from the adjoining estate, his head bent in thought, when she came sailing over the barrier astride a magnificent thoroughbred and reined up beside him.

For a moment she sat her horse regarding him with a bold curiosity. Then she said impatiently, 'Well, don't just stand there gawking like a clod! Help me dismount!'

Just meeting a girl of his own age would have been a disturbing experience. But when the girl also proved to be pretty, poised and scornful, it was devastating.

Donovan stood paralyzed, not knowing what to do or say until, in a pique, she started to dismount. Then he recovered his senses and jumped quickly to help her.

'Well, now, that's better,' she said, mollified, as he set her down. 'I thought for a moment that you must be the stable boy, although I'll admit that I've never seen one quite so big or handsome.'

She was amazingly frank and Donovan felt his ears grow hot with embarrassment.

'I'm sorry,' he said. 'I must seem like a lout to you. But, you see, I've never had a guest before. I'm afraid I don't know how to act.'

'You never had a guest!' The girl's expression was incredulous. 'Why? Don't you like people?'

'It's not that,' Donovan said. 'It's just that no one ever comes to see me.'

A perplexed frown wrinkled the blonde girl's forehead. 'Well, don't you ever go anywhere? I mean to parties and the hunts and things like that?'

Donovan flushed, ill at ease. 'I don't think you understand. I have no friends. I live here alone with Mistress Davies, my tutor, Mrs Ellers, the cook-housekeeper, and Mister Miller, my valet-companion. Two or three times a month I drive into Boston with Mistress Davies or Mister Miller to shop and perhaps go to the theater. The rest of the time...' He shrugged and swept his arm around the estate.

'There are two hundred acres to *Golden Dunes*. Sometimes I hunt, fish, or ride with Mister Miller. Sometimes I read. And sometimes...' he hesitated. 'Sometimes I just think.'

A baffled expression shadowed his visitor's face. 'You're a strange boy,' she said. 'I don't think I've ever met anyone like you before.' Then with a bright smile, she held out her hand.

'I'm Constance Farrington. My father is president of Farrington, Dickens, Blake and Colby, Investment Brokers. We've just purchased *The Cove.*

'Now, sir, what is your name?'

Somehow, he managed to answer. 'Donovan.'

'Donovan what?'

He colored. 'Just Donovan.'

'I mean – what is your father's name?'

It was the moment he had dreaded all his life, the question he had always known he would someday be asked. He had often wondered what he would say when it happened. He need not have worried. The answer popped out as easily as a grape pulp.

'I don't have a father.'

'Nonsense!' Constance Farrington tossed her head impatiently. 'Of course you have a father. Everyone has a father.'

'I haven't.' Head up, eyes steady.

'You mean that you're a bastard?'

He was not shocked. The thought had occurred to him also, but he had discarded it.

'No,' he answered. 'I just don't have a father. Or a mother either.'

'Then you're an orphan.' Gently.

'Maybe. I don't know. No one will tell me anything. It's as though they were hiding some dark secret from me.'

Constance Farrington cocked her blonde

head and regarded him thoughtfully. 'You must be an awfully rich orphan to live in a cottage by yourself with a staff of servants. Who pays for everything?'

The question startled Donovan. He stared at her, amazed by her boldness, impressed by her intelligence. Within minutes after meeting him, she was asking about things which had puzzled him for years.

'I don't know,' he admitted, feeling like a fool.

'You *are* a strange boy.' Constance viewed him with a growing interest. 'You live like a young Lord, you don't know who your father is, or your mother, or whether or not you're a bastard, or who pays for your keep. You don't entertain, you don't go to parties, and you don't have any friends.' Her face softened and a strange tenderness filled her eyes.

'I'll bet you've never even kissed a girl, have you?'

She was a forthright young woman, given to frank expression. Yet she felt a strange mixture of emotions far beyond her years for this handsome boy, already six feet tall, who had so much and yet so little.

Donovan ducked his head. 'So what if I haven't. I'll bet there are lots of things you haven't done!'

When she answered, Constance Farrington's voice was warm and sweet. 'You mustn't be ashamed. To me, it makes you something very special. If you'll let me I'd like to be your...' Her gaze shifted, passing over and beyond him, and her expression altered imperceptibly.

'Good afternoon, sir!'

Even before he turned and saw the great figure standing behind him, Donovan knew who it was. Intuition formed a strong part of his nature. The *presence* did not therefore, surprise him.

He had seen the Master many times from a distance, walking alone in the formal gardens of the main grounds, or riding along the beach in the company of guests. Once, there had been a very beautiful woman with him and Donovan had wondered if perhaps she was his mother. But she never came again and after a while the memory of her faded, and even the Master himself blended into the landscape.

At close range, the master of *Golden Dunes* physically dominated his surroundings. A handsome giant in immaculate linen and fashionably tailored suit, he carried himself with a quiet reserve. His aloofness still made him a romantic figure to both debutante and matron alike.

In this moment, however, he looked neither sad nor romantic. Just cold.

'May I ask how you arrived here, young lady?' His tone was courteous and well modulated, yet there was anger behind it.

The girl flushed. 'Why, over the fence, sir. *Prince Hagar* is a fine jumper. I hope you don't mind, sir.' Then, quickly: 'I'm Constance Farrington. My father only recently purchased *The Cove*. Perhaps you know him, sir. He is...'

Speaking with the same impeccable courtesy, the master of *Golden Dunes* said, 'We entertain few visitors here at the *Dunes*, Miss Farrington, and our guests are by invitation. Since the route by which you arrived is unquestionably the shortest, you have my permission to return to your home the same way. Good day, Miss Farrington.'

Constance Farrington stared at him in outraged humiliation. He had not spoken to her as a child. He would have addressed her father, her mother, or anyone else in the same manner. Her fault lay not in her youth nor in her backyard arrival, but in her very presence here beside Donovan.

Yet why should he resent her? Or deny the

lonely boy the right to have friends? What kind of man would...

Slowly she turned and looked at Donovan, noting the tall, big-boned body, the thick, black hair, the handsome face with its fine gray eyes, and suddenly the truth stood there naked before her.

'You fool!' Her young voice shrilled with passion. *'Don't you know who he is?'*

Donovan stared straight at the master of *Golden Dunes*.

'Yes,' he said evenly. 'I know who he is. I think I've known for a long time but couldn't face the fact that he could be that cruel.'

Until that moment, he had never seen hate in another person's eyes. He saw it now, a glowing flame that never touched the handsome face yet so intense that had it been real it would have destroyed him.

Then it was gone.

Without a word, Charles turned and moved with long, unhurried strides toward the great house.

Watching his retreating back, Donovan experienced no sense of loss, only a vast relief that the long nights, tormented by the mystery of his heritage, were over at last. Now that he had identity he could look forward to the future with new confidence.

Yet that future would not be built as the son of the master of *Golden Dunes*.

Donovan was the only name he had ever had.

He wanted no other.

He looked at Constance Farrington, at her clean young beauty, at the lovely mouth already shaping itself into contrition, and he knew a young boy's sorrow for the sweetness of what might have been, and read in her own grave eyes the same shared realization.

'Oh, Donovan, I'm so sorry!' she cried. 'I should have kept quiet. But it was so obvious, even to the same expression in your eyes. Now I've ruined everything. He'll never let me see you again! I know from the way he acted.'

'It's not your fault,' Donovan said. 'I would have found out sooner or later.'

Silently, he helped her mount. And then out of the loneliness of his life, he cried passionately, 'Remember me, Constance! Remember me!'

'I'll never forget you, Donovan! *Never!*'

She leaned over in her saddle, her long blonde hair brushing his face, and kissed him full on the mouth.

'Remember,' she whispered, 'I was the first!'

Quickly, she wheeled the thoroughbred and put him to the gallop. At the last instant, she lifted him up and over the fence, and that was the way Donovan remembered her. Horse and rider outlined in wonderfully free flight against the late summer sky.

He had known her a bare half hour, yet he was never to forget her.

She was his first love.

He never had another.

The following day, Charles closed the cottage, dismissed the staff and, without seeing the boy, sent Donovan off to Harvard.

Within the month, carpenters came and tore down the cottage and carted away the timbers. Then a landscape architect turned the area into a park of blazing flowers and tall, wind-swept trees and no trace remained at *Golden Dunes* of the boy Donovan.

On July 2, 1863, the same day that Charles died, a young Union cavalry officer took a musket ball in the chest at Gettysburg.

After rendering first aid, a surgeon's mate asked the wounded man, 'What is your name, sir?'

'Donovan.'

'First or last name, sir?'

'Just Donovan.'

'But, sir...'

The Lieutenant's eyes chilled. 'The name, Corporal, is Donovan – period.'

'Yes, sir,' the surgeon's mate said, and did the only thing he could do under the circumstances. He wrote *Donovan, Lt., 3rd Brigade, 3rd Cav.* on a tag and tied it to the wounded officer's tunic. Then he helped load the litter into an ambulance wagon and forgot the matter.

At the base hospital, however, doctors, nurses, orderlies and irate record-keepers fared no better. The matter was finally laid to rest when the War Department confirmed that its records listed a *Donovan, Lt., 3rd Brigade, 3rd Cav.* who did indeed have but one name, whether given or surname said officer had refused to indicate, swearing only that he was a legitimate child and that since no law specifically required that a man have plural names he was not going to invent one merely to satisfy the Army.

Subject officer had been awarded a battle-field commission at Bull Run and had since been twice wounded, twice decorated and twice advanced in rank.

After his discharge from the hospital, Donovan was returned to active duty.

In 1864, he rode with a brigade, commanded by Custer, aiding Sheridan on his raids.

When Custer was given command of the Third Division of Cavalry, Donovan went with him. At the battle of Woodstock, which Custer won, Donovan had his favorite horse shot out from under him but escaped injury.

As a brevet Major, he finished out the war with Custer during those solemn moments at Appomattox.

After Appomattox, he laid aside sabre and uniform, purchased a fine bay and a new Spencer repeating rifle and rode westward.

He did not know that his father had died in '63 or that Boston solicitors were seeking his whereabouts as the sole surviving heir. It would have made no difference. He wanted no part of the huge fortune to which he was legally entitled.

His father had had no son. As far as he was concerned he had had no father. When he was eight years old, a groom had named him after a blooded stallion. Before that, he had had no name other than *boy*, *Young Master* and *Young Sir*.

His father had never called him anything. He had never once even spoken to him.

Donovan was his name. He had no past, no roots, no memories other than of *Prince*

Hagar and Constance Farrington outlined in wondrous free flight against a summer sky.

A degenerate named Chris Envers, by a single, savage act on a Missouri farm, set Donovan's feet upon the bounty hunter trail.

The farmer and his son were lying sprawled in the yard when Donovan rode up. Their bodies were still warm and the blood had not yet congealed.

Inside the house, the woman, her dress bunched up about her hips, was still alive. She lived only long enough to describe the man who had done it.

After burying the family, Donovan took up the killer-rapist's trail. He caught up with his quarry at sundown of the second day. They shot it out at point blank range.

The following afternoon, Donovan dismounted before the sheriff's office in Jefferson City and turned the body over to the law.

Only then did he learn that he had bagged big game. There were *Wanted – Dead or Alive* flyers for Chris Envers in half a dozen states and two Territories. Murder, bank robbery, stagecoach holdups, rape, arson, and torture. Rewards totaled eight thousand, five hundred dollars.

Donovan waited around, collected the money, and then rode on. He had no particular destination, no special goal. Not yet twenty-one, he wanted to 'see the elephant'.

In Colorado Territory, he rode into Central City just as three men ran out of a bank after killing the cashier. He killed one and caught the other two after a mile-long chase.

Twenty-five hundred dollars reward.

He kept riding. There was a restlessness within, a seeking for something which drove him constantly onward. Yet whenever he approached too closely to another human being an inner barrier went up and he withdrew behind it.

He was still, in his own mind, just a name, not yet a person.

Everywhere, he found the country swarming with lawless bands of guerrillas. The James brothers, the Youngers, and many other ex-Quantrill raiders who just couldn't settle down after the shooting had stopped.

The law, wherever there was law, did the best it could, but it could not be everywhere at once. And so the worst of these characters rode almost at will, with no real force to oppose them. Posses they outran until the disgusted lawmen turned homeward. Towns they paralyzed with fear. Citizens fled at sight of them.

Only two groups of men did these murderers, bank robbers, cattle rustlers and horse thieves worry about.

The *Pinkertons* they respected as brave, resourceful men backed by a nation-wide organization. But against the *Pinkerton* agents they always had a chance. For the agents where bound by certain moral principles, as well as by the law itself.

But the one breed they both hated and feared had neither conscience nor principle, concerned itself no more with the law than did those it hunted, and viewed them simply as animals to be hunted down for the reward money.

The bounty hunter.

And so Donovan moved across this land of hate and raw violence, of hunter and hunted, with events almost casually shaping his future.

By '69, he had put the Missouri behind him, left the bay's prints upon the Great Plains, across the Rockies, on to California and the lush Oregon country, across Idaho, Montana, Wyoming, and south once more to Texas and Arizona Territory. Not deliberately hunting but somehow always just happening to run into wanted men. Since this form of 'free justice' proved expensive, he accepted the reward money as a matter of common sense.

In two years he brought in nine men, one with eighty-five hundred dollars and three with five thousand dollar rewards on their heads. He earned a total of twenty-nine thousand dollars.

He was a professional.

Oddly enough, he did not think of himself as such until a diner stalked out of a Denver restaurant one night muttering, 'I'll not sit in the same room with that damned bounty hunter!'

It was his first experience with social ostracism but he knew that it would not be his last. He was branded now. Wherever he went men would shun him as though he were some kind of animal, worse than the men he hunted.

The thought did not greatly disturb him. Loneliness had been his life; and had he not been named after an animal? Why should he mind being considered one?

Thereafter, the dust of his trail wound back and forth across the land, no place in particular, no goal in mind beyond the man at the end of each hunt.

Sometimes, seated before a tiny fire drinking black coffee, he wondered how it had all started and where it would end. The solitude, the ostracism, the thanklessness of it all. Why did he keep at it?

It didn't make sense.

He had been brought up as a gentleman, a Harvard man. As an officer and a hero during the war, he had demonstrated qualities of leadership and initiative. With such a background he could still take his place in the smug, secure world of Boston society and become as powerful a financial figure as Charles before him.

He could, but he wouldn't.

He wanted no part of his father's world. Whatever else he became, he was fiercely determined that he would not be another Charles.

That was what he sought to escape. The fact that he *was* Charles' son; and that save for a single, obsessive hate his father had been a man of great courage, decency and character.

It was a situation, a reality which he could not accept. He could no more view Charles in his true light than Charles had been able to separate him from a single tragic incident.

In the beginning, Donovan took it for granted that he had simply drifted into the role of bounty hunter. But as he grew older he occasionally wondered if perhaps it had not been a deliberate choice.

He believed that Charles, born and raised in a highly civilized 'law and order' society, could never have survived in a raw, violent land. Or have had the courage to become something despised by all decent men.

By choosing such a role himself, he had destroyed his father's image.

So he thought.

He was wrong.

Charles could have survived anywhere, become anything he chose and have succeeded at it, for he and his son were both cut from the same bolt of cloth.

Yet Charles died refusing to accept this fact; and Donovan lived trying to escape it.

Thirteen years later, listening to the roar of the wind outside Pete Simpson's cabin, he was still seeking to escape it.

High up in the mountains, a cloudburst dropped eight inches of rain in two hours, pouring hundreds of freshets down the slopes into Christopher Creek. As its level rose, the creek began to flow more swiftly,

eddying and roiling around rocks and over-
hanging brush.

A section of bank collapsed; a tree toppled
with a crash. Underbrush and driftwood
coming down from above jammed against
it, blocking the channel. Water backed up,
foaming white jets spurted through the
tangled mass. The pressure mounted.

And then a big, fast-moving Ponderosa hit
the jam butt-first.

With a tremendous explosive force the
dam burst, sending the backed-up waters
boiling down into the valley, deepening the
channel and chewing away at the banks as it
swept around the bend behind the ranch
buildings.

Donovan heard it while it was still a mile
away.

*Flash flood! Nightmare to travelers, ruin to
small ranchers. Killer of men, stock and wild
game.*

Instantly, he was down the ladder, three
rungs at a time. Shoving open the door, he
plunged out into the 'night'. Driving wind
and rain buffeted him as he ran toward the
corral, sloshing through mud and water.

He slammed headlong into the corral in
the darkness. Opening the gate, he began
firing his pistol, the sound of the shots tiny

pops in the howling wind. Lightning lit up the horse herd, a dark mass of flying manes and tossing heads, racing about in terror. He worked around behind them, yelling and shooting.

The herd broke for the open gate, stampeding toward the far end of the valley.

Donovan ran for the barn. By the time he reached it water was swirling strongly around his ankles. He threw a glance in the direction of the cabin but could see nothing.

He tried not to think about Tommy Lord.

Inside, he barred the door and climbed quickly to the mow. The floor shook under his feet. The whole structure seemed to have come alive.

As he reached the window, lightning lit up the whole valley and he saw a churning, ten-foot-high solid wall of water sweep around the bend, tossing trees and debris high in the air. Although the main wave never broke, water overflowed the banks and rushed toward the ranch.

A foot-high swell washed through the corral and lapped against the barn before being sucked back into the creek as the great wave swept downstream.

As suddenly as it had come it was gone, leaving the little ranch miraculously spared.

Now there was only the sound of the wind and of the rain drumming on the roof.

Donovan lifted the canvas and checked on the colt. It lay quietly in its hay 'corral', the man's presence giving it a sense of security. Replacing the cover, Donovan reloaded his pistol and then stretched out wearily on the floor.

He could do nothing now but wait.

Tommy Simpson was waiting, too, but for him it was a lot harder. Time drags slowly when every minute is agony.

They had removed the rawhide noose, yanked out the vicious chunks of *cholla*, brushed off the ants, and given him a little water, just enough to keep his kidneys functioning.

But the fire in his stomach had passed down into his intestines creating a new agony. When Bestinez offered him a piece of roasted rattlesnake, he shook his head. His throat was too sore to swallow and his lacerated stomach couldn't have taken food anyhow.

Blood-streaked and filthy, he lay naked on the ground, reconciled now to the fact that he was going to die, but determined that they would not make him scream again. He had done that once and it had almost cost his mother's life. Only Donovan had saved her.

He was still scared, but he wasn't a kid anymore. He'd learned a lot during the past day and a half, mostly how little he knew about people.

For instance, his mother was not perfect as he had thought her to be, yet she was no less his mother because of that. The very fact that she could make mistakes the same as him somehow brought her closer to him.

Then there was this thing about Pete.

He'd always thought you could tell a man's character by the way he looked, talked, and acted. But it wasn't that way at all.

Pete didn't look like much, he talked soft, and you figured he'd run at the first sign of trouble. Yet when real trouble had come Pete had stood fast, cool as branch water, with a rifle in his hand but still remembering how to spare a scared kid's pride.

It was a tormenting thought, but he couldn't help thinking it. *How would Monty have reacted?* Looking back he could not recall his father ever once facing up to anything. Always sneaking out of places in the middle of the night owing people, instead of telling them face to face that he was broke and that he would pay them as soon as he could. Boasting about all the big deals he had swung. Borrowing money he'd known he couldn't pay back. Dragging Ma all over the country, living high sometimes, sometimes not. But never giving her a home and security the way Pete had.

What hurt most was having to admit that his father had never once shown him any love. Never once taken the time to teach him the things that a father usually taught his son.

When his mother had married Pete, he, Tommy, hadn't known how to hunt, fish, ride a horse, track a rabbit, or even how to whittle a stick. He hadn't known anything. Maybe that was why he resented Pete. The rancher had done for him what Monty should have done but never had.

It was a bitter pill to swallow, but he swallowed it, accepting Pete Simpson as the only real father he had ever known.

Donovan he couldn't figure out. He wanted to hate the man. But how could you hate someone who kept risking his life to save your mother? It took guts to run right into the middle of a bunch of 'Paches after a woman who wasn't even yours. 'Course maybe Ma was more Donovan's than she was Pete's. It was too deep for him to understand.

Some things he did understand though. He had been stupid to believe that Donovan's surrender would save him. With Donovan dead, Delcha would simply use him to get at his mother and Pete.

As long as Donovan held out there was hope. Not for him, Tommy – he was already good as dead – but for the rest. If he didn't panic his mother into doing something foolish, Donovan might at least be able to save her.

And so he lay there, tight-lipped, stubborn, a boy rapidly becoming a man, while the sky darkened and thunder rumbled in the distance and Delcha, Pena and seven other 'Paches sat cross-legged on the ground, arguing angrily.

Black, impassive, Delcha's eyes swept the circle, betraying none of his inner frustrations.

They were against him. He could read it in their sullen faces, in the uneasy glances which they cast toward the great storm cloud rushing up from the northwest.

He knew what they were thinking. In this flat meadow, circled by the swift flowing creek, a flash flood plunging down from the mountains could trap and kill them all.

One thought dominated their minds. To jump on their ponies and ride away from this accursed place where so many of their friends had already died. They were sick and tired of a battle which they knew they could not win.

The White Eyes was a devil. He had the cunning of a wolf, the ruthlessness of a *commanchero* and the courage of a grizzly bear. They had shot at him many times. They had twice wounded him. Yet he was still alive and eleven of their number were dead. If the great storm did not kill them, tomorrow the circle would be even smaller.

Let us put our backs to this valley and go home!

It was a yearning in their hearts and a resolve in their minds. Respect for Delcha, who had led them on so many successful raids, had kept them silent for days. But they would remain silent no longer. Either he led them back to the *rancheria* or they would desert him.

Sensing their mood, Delcha wondered if perhaps he should not turn their ponies' heads homeward. True, there would be resentment in the *rancheria* when they returned without Chaco's killer. And much keening of the dead. But a few quick raids upon isolated ranches, prospectors, stages and Mexican sheep herders would soon restore their confidence in him. He knew the minds of his people.

His humiliating defeat here would be forgotten.

But he, *Del-she,* would remember, the pain of it like *cholla* digging into his brain and festering there, giving him no relief.

A great, dark hate seized him, feeding upon his warrior pride. *Let them desert him! Let Pena lead them back whimpering like flogged women! He, Delcha, would stay and do what had to be done.*

Turning his head, he trapped the sly triumph in Pena's eyes and realized that the sub-chief meant to challenge him here and now.

A grim smile crossed his dark face and, watching him, Pena scowled. Around the circle the tension kept building. Pena did not know that Delcha had crushed the ambitions of a half dozen would-be leaders before him. Or that his own scheming showed as plainly on his face as a charcoal map on a piece of white doeskin.

Having read that map, Delcha waited for

precisely the right moment to erase it once and for all. That moment came when lightning struck a tree fifty feet away, riving it down the middle.

Leaping to his feet, Delcha pointed toward the onrushing storm.

'It is too much! The *Thunder Beings* will kill us! We go home!'

The circle disintegrated as men ran, yelling and laughing, for their horses.

Pena sat stunned, his hopes evaporating like water on hot sand. The support which he had enjoyed a moment before was gone. Delcha had toyed with him like a wolf with a young bull. Then with just three words, *We go home*, the chief had destroyed him.

In the *rancheria* they would tell how *Del-she* had made a fool of him and the old men would nod their heads and say that *Del-she* was a great war chief like his father and grandfather before him. The young bucks would scorn him and the prettiest squaws would turn their heads and close their thighs against his love.

The thought was maddening.

He leaped to his feet, whipping up his rifle.

'You say we will go home,' he cried. 'I say you lie! You will lead us away from this place, yes, but you will not take us back to the *rancheria!* You will use the boy to draw the White Eyes into the desert. There you will try and ambush him and more of us will die. I say *No!*'

Moving toward their horses, the band stopped, their faces suddenly still.

Bestinez turned to Delcha. 'Is this true what Pena says? That you will not take us home?'

'Pena twists the truth to serve his own purposes,' Delcha retorted. 'I tell you again – we go home. If the White Eyes follows we will kill him. But we will not go out of our way to hunt him down.'

'You lie!' Pena shouted. 'You are like the feather tribes, the Sioux, the Cheyenne, the Arapahoes. Once they plant the lance they will not turn back, no matter how many of them die. That may be brave, but it is also stupid.'

'You speak like a sheep herder, not an Apache,' Delcha taunted. 'I say if you are afraid, go home and sit with the women.'

It was the ultimate insult, deliberately cast.

As Pena raised the rifle, Delcha shot him in the chest, killing him instantly.

Silently the group turned away and moved

toward their horses.

'He was an Apache and a brave man,' Delcha called after them. 'Would you leave him here for the buzzards? Tie him on his pony, Bestinez. He wanted to go back to his own *rancheria*. We will...'

A rolling crash of thunder drowned out his words. They heard the moaning roar of the storm rushing down from the mountains and each read in his friend's face the terror of supernatural forces against which he could not fight.

Wind, who whispered softly in men's ears and then without warning flattened wickiups and blew away entire rancherias... Thunder Beings whose flint-tipped shafts of lightning flamed down out of the sky to split trees, explode rocks, and kill men... He Who Controls Water, who dressed in a shirt of colored clouds and caused the rains ... and Water Monster, a terrible creature in serpent form who inhabited lakes and streams and drowned animals and people, White Eyes and Apache alike.

Aiieee! The terror was upon them!

Quick, hard gusts batted their faces. The first large raindrops thinned the blood running from Pena's chest as he lay face down across his pony's back.

In the eerie light men could barely recognize one another at arm's length.

Panic-stricken, a brave leaped for his pony.

'No!' Delcha shouted. 'Run for the barn! Bestinez, bring the boy! We'll come back for the horses!'

He had to shout above the roar of the wind as it tore through the trees.

In single file they ran through the timber, slamming into pinons, stumbling over underbrush in the dim light. A smothering torrent of rain struck them just as they reached the creek, half drowning them. It was like trying to breathe under water, with the wind forcing the rain up their nostrils and into their open mouths.

Slipping, falling on the smooth stones of the creek bottom, they waded across with the quickening current pulling at their ankles. Bestinez, with Tommy Lord slung over his shoulder, was the last to reach the opposite bank.

There they huddled together, their teeth chattering, until a flash of lightning showed them the dim bulk of the barn behind the rain curtain. Then they dashed across the clearing.

They had but one thought now – the shelter of the barn, out of this howling fury.

The first to reach the barn, Delcha yanked

at the big door. It did not budge. At first he thought the wind was holding it closed. But when all of them together could not open it, he realized that it was barred from the inside.

A helpless fury seized him. No matter what he did the White Eyes always anticipated him. He had been certain the barn would be empty. But Donovan must have guessed he would seek shelter there and had locked himself inside.

'What do we do now?' Bestinez shouted.

'See if you can find a ladder!'

With Bestinez beside him, he groped his way around in the darkness beneath the mow window.

Suddenly a near-blinding flash of lightning lit up the clearing and Delcha saw the massive figure of the White Eyes standing in the mow window, rifle in hand, looking down at them.

'Run!' he shouted, and heard his voice as a tiny, muted sound in the void. 'Back to the horses!'

Halfway across the creek, he ducked at the crack of the Winchester being rapidly fired from the barn.

Even in the midst of all this hell the White Eyes was still trying to kill him!

Delcha shivered and for the first time doubt flowed through his mind.

At the start, they had thought of it as a game. Twenty hot-blooded warriors running down a lone White Eyes as though he were a rabbit. Now it was no longer a game. On this twenty-third day of the chase only seven of the twenty who had so confidently started out were still alive. And still Donovan, although wounded, was as dangerous as ever.

Truly *Coyote* was roaming the land, stirring up trouble for the Apaches!

Somehow they found their horses, neighing and plunging around the clearing. Mounting, they waited while Bestinez tied the young White Eyes on his pony. Then they wheeled and worked their way through the timber to the open country beyond.

There the full force of the storm struck them, threatening to blow them off their horses. Rain, coming down harder now, stung their faces like sleet. A man could not see his friend at ten feet. They kept bumping into one another, their horses slipping and floundering in the hock-deep mud.

Within minutes the group had hopelessly scattered.

In the lightning-speared darkness men reined up, terrified by the realization that they were out here alone with *He Who Controls Water* and *Water Monster* and that if they stayed...

Moccasined heels thudded against ponies' flanks.

Southward they fled, not caring if a horse stepped in a gopher hole and broke a leg or its rider's neck. Not caring about anything but getting back to the *rancheria* alive.

Bestinez, leading Tommy Lord's pony, reined up to get his bearings just as lightning hit a tree a dozen feet away. The Apache's horse reared, almost throwing him. Fighting to control the animal he dropped the reins of Tommy Lord's pony. Immediately the terrified creature bolted into the darkness.

Bestinez swore. Delcha would be furious over the young White Eyes' escape, but there was no help for it. Not even *Water Monster* could find the boy in this storm.

Savagely he swung the pinto and with the storm at his back headed southward.

Twenty feet away Delcha, also riding south, pulled up as a fast-traveling rider crashed through the oak brush to his right. He called out but there was no answer and in a moment the sound died away.

No matter, he thought. The rider would find his way to the cave rendezvous near the source of Tonto Creek. Apaches always had at least two pre-arranged meeting places in case they became separated or had to retreat in battle.

He kneed his horse into motion, resentful of the chill in his thighs which made it difficult for him to keep his seat. He wondered if *he* would live to reach the rendezvous.

Although he had no wish to die just yet, he was not afraid. At least he was not afraid of *Man Who Controls Water* or *Water Monster;* and he was only a little afraid of *Coyote.*

What he did fear was that he might die before he killed the White Eyes.

By *Ysun, the Giver of Life,* he was glad they had the boy! With the young White Eyes as bait they could draw the bounty hunter south into the desert where they could get at him. Then, if *Coyote* wanted to take away what *Ysun* had given, he, Delcha, would not mind.

For twenty-three days he had pursued Donovan all over Arizona Territory. Now Donovan would have to chase him. Only he wouldn't be running. He would be patiently waiting for the right time and the right place to strike.

Aiieee!

He threw back his head and laughed, half

choking as rain poured into his mouth, but not minding at all.

To Tommy Lord the storm was simply more terror added to a day and night of mounting violence.

Battered by wind and pelted by a cold, stinging rain, he submitted to being tied on a pony with a dull indifference. He guessed that they were taking him away from the ranch, maybe back to their own *rancheria*. He didn't care anymore so long as they left his mother and Pete alone.

But if they counted on Donovan coming after him, they were wrong. Donovan wouldn't. Why should he risk his life for a big-mouthed, smart-alec kid?

No, Tommy Lord was a goner. He might as well face up to that fact.

A rider crowded alongside and grabbed his pony's bridle. In a moment, the entire band moved out, horses rearing and skittering around and plunging into one another and men cursing in angry frustration.

For a while, Tommy Lord caught glimpses of them whenever lightning flashed. Then suddenly they were all gone save for the man leading his horse.

The 'Pache reined up and Tommy Lord

sensed his fear of being separated from the others. He wondered if the man might panic and ride away and leave him. Much as he wanted to escape, he did not want to be abandoned in this storm with his hands tied and his feet roped beneath his pony's belly.

As he started to knee closer to Bestinez, lightning hit a tree only yards away. He saw the 'Pache's horse rear up, its forefeet pawing the air, and Bestinez bent forward trying to bring it down.

Then his own mount exploded under him in headlong flight. Grabbing the pony's mane with his bound hands he clamped his legs tight and held on as it tore through the oak brush. Branches ripped his naked body, already blistered by sun, torn by *cholla*, and welted by rawhide. Once the pony stumbled and he thought, *He's goin' to roll on me an' bust me to pieces*. But luck was with him.

Laying his head against the straining animal he fought to ride it out.

No one could help him now.

No one.

By eight o'clock the storm had subsided to a steady rain that beat monotonously upon the barn roof.

Through a gun port Donovan saw a faint

213

glow of light from the cabin and knew that the Simpsons had also weathered the blow.

He would have liked a hot meal but decided against it. The woman would use him to taunt her husband; and Simpson, already in a dangerous mood, would likely not put up with it.

There was no point in stirring up trouble.

His immediate concern was Tommy Lord. Weakened by torture and exposure the boy could not survive much more punishment. Time was running out on him.

Donovan rolled a cigarette and leaned back to think things over. He was certain that Delcha had left the area to escape the storm. By now the band was probably holed up somewhere along Tonto Creek.

When the storm passed Delcha would move out, making sure to leave plenty of sign until the land opened up and there was no chance of the White Eyes escaping.

Then he would strike.

It was, Donovan conceded, logical and foolproof. He had not been able to stand and fight them in the open before. Even with their number now cut in half, he could still not hope to do so. He could follow, but he could not close in and rescue the boy. Unless...

Inevitably, it came back to that. The one slim hope which he had held forth to Peggy Simpson without revealing details.

He was convinced that were he dealing with a 'feather' Indian – a Sioux, Cheyenne, or Arapahoe – the plan would work. A Plains Indian was more than a warrior; he was a proud, fierce man to whom personal courage ranked above all else, and who was prepared to die to prove his own.

But an Apache was a different breed. He did not seem to have the dignity, the self-respect, or the sense of values that characterized the Sioux, for instance.

Perhaps, however, that was because he did not know them as well. Certainly Chaco had been a brave man. Brave enough to die rather than submit to the white man's law. And then there was Victorio, Geronimo, Cochise, Nachez and, doubtless, many others.

But was Delcha one of them? He had no choice but to gamble and find out.

He rose and went to the mow window. Rain still fell steadily and lightning flickered far away. He took a last drag on the cigarette and flipped it into the night.

A faint snicker from the hay 'corral' reminded him of the colt. He could not remember whether or not the mare was still in the barn. Throwing back the trap, he picked up the colt and awkwardly descended the ladder.

By the time he reached the bottom, the mare was there, waiting. He set the colt down and almost immediately heard it noisily sucking its mother's teats.

He was smiling when he stretched out on the floor of the mow, his rifle beside him, and fell asleep.

Fifty yards away, Pete and Peggy Simpson lay staring up at the ceilings of different rooms, drained of all emotion save bitterness, waiting out the long night without hope for Tommy, for themselves, or for the future if they survived.

A rooster crowing outside awakened Donovan. He lay there, his mind absorbing, identifying the night sounds. The faint slapping of a loose shingle ... the mare moving about in her stall below ... a mocking bird trilling from the big oak ... the shrill yapping of half a dozen coyotes from the timber across the creek. Normal sounds.

He had slept seven hours, more uninterrupted sleep than he had had in a month. He felt alert, ready to move out.

He rose, brushed the hay from his hair, and went down the ladder.

The colt was nursing again, its lip-smacking noisy signs of contentment.

Opening the door, he stepped outside. The rain had stopped and, save for a few fast-drifting clouds, the sky was clear. A pale silver slice of moon hung in the west, with dawn still an hour away.

Donovan shivered in the chill air, reminded that here in the mountains snow was not unusual in late September. From now on, the heat would begin to drop, with the afternoon west wind growing cooler, until one morning the horses would have to break through a thin film of ice in the watering trough to drink.

He looked up at the sky and wondered if he would be alive when that happened.

Impatiently, he thrust the thought aside.

Carrying a *riata*, he walked slowly toward the corral. It was empty. The horse herd was still in the meadow. He would have to go after them.

As he passed the big oak, he saw a light burning in the cabin's kitchen. He hesitated, then turned and walked toward it. If Simpson heard him out there in the dark, he might shoot him for an Apache.

He stopped and called out, 'Simpson!'

The rancher answered immediately. 'What's wrong?'

'I'm going out to rope a horse. I didn't want to get shot for an Apache.'

'Are you leaving?'

'Yes.'

A long pause. 'You'd better take the gray. He's the fastest. I'll have Peggy fix you some breakfast.'

In the darkness, Donovan shook his head. Simpson was quite a man in a lot of ways. It was too bad his wife could not see that.

'Thanks,' he said, and moved away.

It was tough going through the meadow, with his boots sinking into the mud and the long, wet grass dragging at his legs.

The herd loomed up ahead of him, a dark mass in the starlight. Speaking soft, he moved among them, searching for the gray. It was not hard to find. Even for a racer bred to outrun ordinary horses while hauling a stage coach, the gray was something special.

My God, he's big! Donovan thought. Seventeen hands. Thirteen hundred pounds anyway. Long in leg, neck and barrel. Deep-chested. Powerful hindquarters. A stallion, proud, spirited.

A damn big, beautiful horse needing a big,

powerful man to handle him.

Standing there with his head lifted, sniffing the wind, he reminded Donovan of another stallion in an all but forgotten time. Equally big, powerful, and spirited, who had died without ever having known the touch of steel or leather.

Other than his wife, the stallion *Donovan* was the only thing Charles had ever loved.

And other than Constance Farrington, the stallion had been the only creature who had ever come close to the man who bore his name.

In this moment, save for the years, Donovan might well have been standing in the paddock of *Golden Dunes* talking to a horse dead now for almost a quarter of a century.

'I need you, you big, beautiful bastard,' he said softly. 'I may have to burst your lungs and break that great heart of yours wide open. But that's what you were bred for ... to keep going after the crow-bait drops. You're a thoroughbred, and don't you ever forget it! Now, come here.'

The stallion's ears perked and he trotted to the man without hesitation. Sensing the strength, the mastery, he took Donovan's great weight easily, submitting without loss of pride or independence. By the time they reached the cabin, they were no longer horse and rider, master and beast, but equals, working and sharing together.

Putting the stallion in the corral, away from the mare, Donovan went to the barn for his saddle.

The stallion took leather as quietly as he had the man. Simpson knew how to train horses. Donovan knew how to make them love him.

The sky was paling in the east when Donovan walked toward the cabin.

In the kitchen, Pete Simpson set down his coffee cup and motioned Donovan to a chair. The rancher's face was haggard, his eyes red-rimmed from lack of sleep.

'Sit,' he said. 'Breakfast will be ready in a minute.'

Standing at the stove, with her back to them, Peggy Simpson gave no indication that she had heard, but the rigidity of her body, the high-held head betrayed her.

Donovan sat down; and after a moment, she came over with the coffee pot and filled his cup, not looking at him, her mouth sullen, her face drawn into tight lines of hostility.

'Thanks,' Donovan said.

Without replying, she went back to the stove, heaped a platter with bacon and eggs and brought them to him. She started to say something. Her mouth quivered. She turned quickly away, brushing at her eyes with the back of her hand.

She would always touch Donovan with this quiet show of courage, so different from her violent flare-ups.

'Your son is still alive,' he said compassionately. 'I saw him less than seven hours ago.'

Simpson cleared his throat. 'I thought I heard firing last night. What happened?'

'They tried to get in out of the storm,' Donovan said. 'I had the door locked. A big flash of lightning lit up everything. When they saw me standing in the mow, they ran. I fired a few shots over their heads to keep them going.'

'Was that when you saw Tommy?'

Donovan nodded. 'He was slung over the shoulder of an Apache named Bestinez. I met Bestinez once on the San Carlos reservation. He's not quite as bad as the rest.'

Peggy Simpson swung around, her eyes brimming. 'How do you know he wasn't already dead?'

'Bestinez wouldn't have been carrying a

corpse around in that weather,' Donovan said. 'The boy was alive, all right.'

Peggy Simpson searched the big man's face intently. Then she spoke with a restrained composure.

'Well, now that they've gone, you can ride away scot-free. It doesn't matter what happens to Tommy, does it?'

She went to the pantry, picked up a sack of food and, coming back, put it on the table in front of him.

'You saved my life twice,' she said. 'I'd give anything if you hadn't. It's hard to feel obligated to someone you hate. Now, for God's sake, get on your horse and ride away from here!'

Draining his coffee cup, Donovan rose, picked up his rifle and the grub sack, and walked to the door. There he turned, his face impassive, and looked at her.

'You don't owe me a thing!'

He was gone.

Pete Simpson put down his coffee cup with a tired gesture. He gave his wife a long, free glance.

'You shouldn't have talked to him that way.'

'Oh, shut up!'

'You know where he's headed?'

Peggy Simpson's lip curled. 'Back to Tucson where it's safe!'

'No; he's going after Tommy.'

'I don't believe it!' she cried. 'He wouldn't risk his life for anyone!'

Simpson's eyes held steady. 'He risked it for you.'

Peggy flushed. 'That was different.'

'Because he loves you?' Simpson rose and went over to the ammunition shelf. Methodically, he began filling his cartridge belt.

'I thought that, too, at first,' he said. 'Now I know he'd have done it if you'd been a squaw and ninety years old.'

'You don't know him!' Peggy stormed. 'He's bad clear through!'

Emptying his .45, Simpson punched in fresh shells. His face took on a pinched expression.

'No one's all bad or good,' he said. 'That's your trouble. You keep hunting for the perfect man. When are you going to realize he don't exist?

'Because I didn't measure up you struck back at me by sleeping with Donovan. Now that makes you something less than perfect yourself. But does it make you a whore? I called you that, but I was wrong. It just makes you human, like me and the rest of the world.'

Holstering the .45, he jacked the shells out of the Winchester and took down a fresh box of ammunition. Suddenly he paused, his face softening.

'Sometimes people do foolish things in anger. Afterward, it's too late to make up for them. Whatever you've done ought to be settled between you and your conscience, not between you and me.'

He thumbed the last shell into the rifle. Then stuffing bread and meat into a bag he went out, leaving her standing there.

A sudden panic seized Peggy Simpson. Behind Pete's words she sensed a final decision.

He was leaving her.

Two years ago she wouldn't have cared. Six months ago she wouldn't have minded too much. But to be rejected twice in a single day...

'Pete!' She ran out into the yard. 'Pete, wait!'

He hesitated, then kept going. A moment later, he disappeared into the barn.

She stood there, angry and afraid, knowing that he would return, but not knowing exactly what to say or do when he did. What he had told her was true. Some of it she had already admitted to herself. Now the rest of it was beginning to surface.

If she had hurt Pete, she had hurt herself far more. To know that he had once loved her deeply, and now to have him look at her as though she were a stranger...

A great, aching sense of loss grew inside her, expanding until she felt that she could no longer bear it. Yet she would have to learn to live with it for it would be with her always.

Pete came out of the barn carrying his saddle and a hackamore. He hung the saddle on a corral pole and came toward her, rifle slung in the crook of his arm.

'Pete!' She reached out and caught his arm. 'Where are you going?'

'To help Donovan.'

Still holding his arm, she walked along beside him, trying to match her stride to his but having trouble because the wet grass kept dragging at her dress and holding her back.

'Pete, do you really think he's gone after Tommy?'

'Yes.'

'How can you be so sure?'

'Because I know Donovan. If it was me

instead of Tommy he'd still go. Or if it was someone he'd never even heard of. Don't ask me to try and explain him. I can't. I wish to God I could. But somewhere along the line, he had a choice between hating the world or caring what happened to people.'

They were coming up now on the herd and Simpson began to uncoil his *riata*. The sky had lightened and when he stopped and turned toward her, Peggy could see the tenseness of his face.

'There's something I've got to tell you,' he said. 'Maybe if I'd told you at the beginning things might have worked out differently. I don't know.'

'What are you talking about?' Peggy said.

'I knew who he was the minute he told me his name,' Simpson replied. 'I'd heard stories about him in Tucson three years ago. He was a legend even then.'

It was difficult for him and, sensing it, Peggy squeezed his arm and said quietly, 'Go on.'

'He was a boy Major in the Union cavalry during the war. A hero. After Appomattox he rode westward like thousands of other men. He always seemed to be around when trouble started. Afterward, he'd find out that he'd either captured or killed a man with a price on his head. Naturally, he accepted the reward. Pretty soon it became a job.'

Peggy Simpson remained motionless, saying nothing, while her husband brushed aside the mystery surrounding the man who had turned her life upside down.

'He's known throughout the west. Dodge City, Abilene, San Antonio, The Nations, Denver, Salt Lake, Cheyenne, Pendleton, Sioux City, Walla Walla, San Francisco – and, of course, all over Arizona Territory.

'He's brought in almost a hundred men, killed six, got a couple acquitted he thought were innocent, and collected a quarter of a million dollars in bounties.

'Except for Chaco, he gave the men he killed Christian burial at his expense. The Apache he left where his own people could find him.'

As he hesitated, Peggy urged him on. 'What else do you know about him?'

Simpson frowned, not wanting to but just the same feeling jealous of her interest in Donovan. It surprised him. He had thought that she could no longer touch him. She could and she had.

He shrugged. 'By his talk, he's from some-where East. When he's in town, they say he dresses like an gentleman, lives in the best hotels, eats at fancy restaurants, and goes to concerts and lectures and things like that. It's rumored he comes from a very rich family.'

'I guessed all that,' Peggy said impatiently. 'But what about Donovan the *man?*'

Uneasily, Simpson looked at the sun. He ought to be on his way. However, with the ground still wet, tracking would be easy. And Donovan wouldn't travel fast until the sun had warmed the stallion's muscles.

He relaxed, deciding to humor Peggy, but having the odd feeling that it was she who was drawing all of this out of him against his will.

'Well, like I told you, he likes the good life. But he doesn't throw his money away. Average drinker, plays a few hands of poker now and then, no sprees with fancy women. Oh, he has affairs; but he draws his women from high society and nothing ever comes from it.'

Peggy stared at him blankly. 'You mean he doesn't even keep a mistress! Then what does he do with all his money?'

'No one knows for sure,' Simpson replied. 'But it's common knowledge that he's supported Carmelia Ortega, the widow of a man he shot by mistake, for the past seven years. They say her son, Victorio, is a genius with a guitar and that Donovan plans to send him to Spain to study.

'A lot of his money seems to go to mission orphanages and to big medical centers. He's got this something about kids that nobody can figure out. A doctor in Tucson claims Donovan pays him fifty dollars every time he delivers a baby under nine pounds – *if* he can explain how he kept its weight down during pregnancy. It don't make sense to me, but that's what he said.'

It made sense to Peggy Simpson. Donovan was a giant of a man. He must also have been a very large baby. Sometimes a woman died trying to give birth a such a child.

She would, of course, never know the truth, but she thought she could guess what had happened. Or at least a part of it.

The mother had died.

The father had hated.

The child had endured.

The 'man' had pushed it from his mind save for the guilt-feeling about his mother. Having suffered he had learned compassion.

But Donovan was no milk-sop idealist. From the very first, she had sensed within him a natural violence. A violence constantly warring against a deeply ingrained humanism.

Like herself, Peggy thought, he was both good and bad, so evenly balanced that he could go one way or the other, depending upon the situation.

A 'loner', he liked people, at least some people. Kind, he could be merciless. A killer, he saved people's lives.

He was a paradox; and it was this similarity in their natures that had first drawn them together. And it was this similarity which still held her to him against her will.

'...With no close friends,' Pete was saying. 'He keeps people at a distance. Minds his own business, never starts trouble. But nobody is fooled. He's a dangerous man. A dark, moody man sometimes.

'No two people feel the same way about him. He's liked, respected, feared and hated. I don't think he cares one way or the other. He doesn't need anyone. They say...'

'They say! They say!' Angrily, Peggy Simpson flung off her husband's arm. 'Rumor, gossip, hearsay! What do any of them really know about him? Nothing!

'What about *before* the war? Where was he born? What town, what state? Who were his parents, and what were they like? Why does he have only one name? Did he have a pet, a dog, a squirrel? Was he a good student and did his classmates like him? Who was his first love? Does he still remember her?'

The words poured out of her in a questioning flood. She was seeking desperately to know the *totality* of a man.

'Did he dream as a youth?' she cried. 'Does he *still* dream? About how, about what? Why is he maybe riding to his death to try and save a boy who hates him? You say because it's natural to him. But what is "natural"? Tell me, and I'll know Donovan! Otherwise, I'll never know who he was, what he was, or why he was! Or the *why* of me!'

It was this *Why of me?* that drove her. Already Donovan had freed her of the doll. Yet she realized now that the doll had been only a red herring drawn across her mind to hide a deeper truth. Whatever that truth was, it kept evading her. So she knew that it could not be pleasant. But until she exposed it, she would never find happiness with any man.

Donovan was the key.

If what she suspected about his life was true, then it was, indirectly, a reflection of her own. With possibly one exception.

Donovan had overcome the hate, the

rejection, the loneliness without hating in return.

Had she, too? Or was she still driven by...

'...Jealous. I was afraid to be compared to a man like Donovan. Now do you understand why I didn't tell you at first?'

Pete's voice erased the thought which had almost reached the surface of her mind.

She studied his thin face, splashed now by the sun's light, and wondered at the sudden gentleness which filled her. A week ago, her growing feeling for him had still been colored with contempt and pity. Emotions which she knew she could never again experience toward him.

He did not deserve contempt. He was above pity.

During the past two days, she had observed a Pete Simpson to whom she had been blind for four years. A man who had reacted to danger with a cool, quick decisiveness. A man who, under great emotional stress, had shown an even greater kind of courage.

In the end, it had been her own shameless arrogance that had killed his love for her. Even so, he still gave her a consideration which hurt far more than had that single open-handed blow.

Mistaking her silence, Pete Simpson

started to turn away; but she stopped him with a wordless motion of her hand.

'Yes, I can understand,' she said evenly. 'Perhaps if I had known at the beginning I might have acted differently. I don't know.

'All I know is that my son is out there somewhere in terrible danger, and that I keep forgetting him because of my own troubles. Maybe it's because I can't really think of him as still being alive. Maybe I've already given him up for dead. And now I'm trying to put him out of my mind to keep from going mad. Do you think I'm mad, Pete?'

'No.' Simpson measured her with a penetrating glance. 'You bend, but you'll never break.'

Moving in among the herd, he selected a speedy bay, slipped on the hackamore, and started back toward the cabin.

'Pete!' Peggy ran after him. 'Let me go with you!' Then, quickly, before he could object. 'They might just be trying to draw you and Donovan away from the ranch. If they should circle and find me alone...'

Simpson halted, his face growing grave. He hesitated, rubbing his chin thoughtfully. Then he nodded.

'All right.' He handed her the hackamore rope. 'Ride back and saddle up. Pack a bedroll, a poncho, a canteen, and grub for a couple of days. Take the other rifle and plenty of ammunition. I'll be along in a minute.'

He boosted her on the bay and slapped its rump.

She went away from him at the gallop, having, for the first time, a sense of purpose and meaningful direction.

Her son was somewhere out there in the dawn.

Two men cared enough to risk their lives to save him.

Maybe Pete and Tommy didn't care for her anymore because of what she had done, but she cared for them. She cared for them all: Tommy, Pete, Donovan.

The thought swept over her like last night's storm, sudden, frightening. It seemed incredible that this thing should happen to her. For she realized now that she had never before loved anyone in her life. Even her feeling for Tommy had been a kind of self-love.

Love was dangerous. It could destroy you. It took your pride, your self-respect, your will, and left you nothing but pain and loneliness.

As a little girl, she had learned that. She had loved her mother and her mother had

called her an 'unnatural' child. She had
loved her father and her father had rejected
her. He had been too busy preaching about
his God of vengeance, too busy with his own
secret hates to be able to love.

He had been successful at only one thing
in his whole miserable life; hating, arousing
hate, and spreading hate.

You twisted, sanctimonious hypocrite! she
thought. *I hate your guts! I've hated you all my
life, but wouldn't admit it. You weak, vicious,
sordid excuse for a father!*

And so it came out of her in a violent,
bitter flood that had been unconsciously
held back all her life. As it did, she began to
understand the sickness within her which
had all but destroyed her.

Honor they father and thy mother.

Children couldn't hate their fathers; so
she'd had to pretend to hate someone else.
She'd hated every man she had ever met,
and probably Monty most of all.

Children couldn't strike back at their
fathers, even after they grew up. So she'd
had to find a whipping boy.

She had found Pete Simpson, who had
loved her enough to ignore her past, give her
and her son a home and love and who had
asked for so little in return. He hadn't even

235

gotten that. All she had ever given him had been contempt, ingratitude and, as a final blow, betrayal.

Yet every hurt, every humiliation, every outrage had been a blow not at Pete but at a long dead father whom she had never been able to punish in life and who had long ago escaped her through death.

In this moment, it all became so very clear to her. But it was already far too late. She had lost Pete. She had never really had Donovan. And she had probably lost Tommy.

It was a terrible price to pay for having found herself. Yet if it had to be paid she would pay it.

A sudden sense of exultation engulfed her. She lifted her face to the morning sun and gave the bay its head and went racing across the meadow, her long black hair streaming in the wind and her heart pounding for the first time with the sheer joy of living.

Tommy could die; she could die; they could all die. It wouldn't matter. What mattered was that for the first time in her life she cared for another human being – and was not afraid.

Mane-riding a fleet sorrel far behind her, Pete Simpson saw her turn and wave and with a strange lightening of the heart, he waved back.

Half an hour later, the two of them rode away from the ranch, heading south at a fast clip.

Delcha was in a killing mood.

Kneeling before a wind-eroded 'window' of the tiny lookout niche, he stared blackly across the sweeping land to the northwest.

Loss of the young White Eyes had all but wiped out his last hope of taking Donovan. With the boy safe, the bounty hunter would simply outrun them to Tucson. He had a thoroughbred racer to do it with now.

By *Ysun*, why had Bestinez let the boy escape! Yet despite his resentment, he knew that Bestinez had not been at fault. Some of that resentment was also against himself. For in those first moments of anger, he had forgotten that Bestinez had been his friend for many years. He had said things that should not have been said. He had humiliated his friend before others.

Bestinez had stood silent, his face taking on the cast of dark red granite. Then he had turned and walked away, leaving the ashes of their friendship behind him.

He was an Apache; he would not forget.

For what had happened, Delcha blamed

himself, Bestinez, *Water Monster,* the *Thunder Beings,* and *Coyote.* But, most of all, he blamed Donovan. Although he hated all White Eyes, he reserved for the bounty hunter that special hatred accorded a deadly enemy. By now, Donovan had become a mystic symbol of the future. If he could destroy the White Eyes, then he could destroy the future. He believed this with a fanatic intensity.

He frowned, squinting up at the high noon sun. The boy, provided he was still alive, could not have gone far. Nor, bound as he was, could he have guided the horse back to the cabin. Bestinez and Seca should have found him and been back an hour ago.

A hundred feet below, one of the braves squatting in front of the cave yelled with laughter. The whole band was happy. They were going home. Relaxed, well-fed, they waited for Bestinez to return with the young White Eyes. Then they would be on their way.

Delcha's mouth twisted with disgust. *Women! Good only to slit the throats of Mexican sheep herders! Not one fit to ride with a raiding party.*

He felt suddenly very lonely, aware that he was a part of the last days of the Apache. He thought of his father, killed by one of Gray Wolf's soldiers, and of his grandfather, who had ridden with *Magnus Colorado* and, had died on a raid into New Mexico. Of his little brother, whose name he could no longer remember, running toward him, screaming, with the diamondback's fangs still buried in his face. It had been in the middle of his fourth summer.

Other faces crowded in upon him now, friend and enemy, to remind him of how quickly the seasons passed. His wife, Bonita, dead of smallpox a dozen years. His sons, too young to fight, who would end up like sheep on a reservation.

Chaco, a chief who had known how to die; Pena, brave but not wise; Bestinez, whose heart had turned against him; Nachez, second son of Cochise; Geronimo; and wild, fierce Victorio, who were turning Arizona, New Mexico and Sonora into a bloody hunting ground.

A few vivid personal memories, too. His first battle, an attack on a party of fifteen miners in the Superstitions ... the big man with the flaming red beard, almost as red as the blood gushing from his mouth as *Del-she's* arrow passed through his lungs... His first woman, who had taught him that there were ways other than the warpath to conquer a man... The mouth-watering smell of fresh killed mule roasting over the flames.

Lying on his back, staring up at the stars and thinking of *Ysun, the Giver of Life,* who had created the Universe... *White Painted Woman,* who had existed 'from the beginning'... *Child of Water* and *Killer of Enemies, White Painted Woman's* sons, who met and slew many of the monsters who bothered the Earth People ... the *Gan,* the Mountain People, who lived on top of mesas and in caves and who, wishing to avoid the death that inevitably came to human beings, had left to seek a world of eternal light ... the *Water People... Coyote,* who brought to man such undesirable things as death, gluttony, thievery, adultery and lying...

Of feeling all around him the presence of the souls of all things: sun, moon, thunder, wind, lightning, tree, rock, bird, Man, himself...

Delcha sighed. The old days were gone. Even the present was galloping into the past like a frightened pony. The future he did not wish to see, with the White Eyes covering the mountains and deserts like swarms of deer flies.

Aiieee!

It was a time for dying and he would not have it otherwise. Let him live only long enough to kill this devil, Donovan, who was destroying his faith in himself as a man, and as an Apache. After that, let *Coyote* slip into his *wickiup*. He would not care.

Ysun, White Painted Woman, or *Child of Water,* who some claimed had made Man from mud or clouds, could send him to the Shadowland. He had lived thirty-six summers. They were enough for...

A dazzling light struck him in the eyes, flashing back and forth across the face of the lookout niche.

He thought at first that it was an Army heliograph 'talking'. But then he remembered that they had seen no sign of troops in more than two weeks. And Apaches did not use the 'talking' mirrors.

His eyes swept the land far out to the northwest.

The light hit him in the face, half blinding him. He jerked his head aside. The light followed.

He sighted along the Winchester barrel, trying to focus on it.

Like a humming bird, the light darted back and forth, around and around, stabbing at his eyes.

Delcha cursed softly. Someone was out there with field glasses deliberately taunting him, wanting him to know where they were.

The light vanished, then reappeared some six hundred yards out, pin-pointing two horsemen moving slowly toward the look-out.

Resting his rifle on the wind-slot, Delcha watched the riders approach. Even before they came within range, he knew who they were. And that they were dead.

With a strangled cry, he emptied the Winchester at his unseen enemy.

Immediately, the light whipped back, forcing him to drop to his knees to escape it.

The hunter had become the hunted.

The White Eyes had issued a challenge.

He had made it clear, however, that he was not going to be drawn into a trap. He would stay out of range and wait, taunting them with the mirror, playing upon their pride as warriors until they came at him on a battlefield of his own choosing.

He now had to run to maneuver, to outrun them on the racer, or to pick them off one at a time from a distance. It was like the beginning of the chase, with one exception. He had reduced the odds against him by half, shattered their confidence, and set them against one another.

Nevertheless, his own position was still very dangerous. He was outnumbered five to one. He was wounded, how badly Delcha did not know. And he had to sleep, whereas some Apaches could constantly be seeking him out, harassing him.

Delcha frowned. Something was not right. With field glasses, Donovan must know that they did not have the boy. Why then did he choose to fight instead of riding safely back to Tucson?

Below, he heard men yelling as the horses bearing the bodies of Bestinez and Seca trotted into camp. He shut out the sound, his mind busy with the thought that kept nagging him.

Why? Unless there was something to gain. What? Time. Why would he be stalling for time? He didn't need...

A slow smile spread Delcha's lips.

The boy, of course.

Bestinez and Seca had not found him. Donovan had cut their trail and killed them. But neither had he been able to find the young White Eyes. That meant the boy had control of his horse, was covering his tracks, and heading for home.

Realizing that the entire band would soon

be joining in the search, Donovan had ridden here with his flashing mirror and his arrogant courage to distract them.

Like the quail drawing the hunter away from its young, he would taunt them until the young hotheads took off in angry pursuit forgetting the boy. Then he would give the thoroughbred its head and run them into the ground miles away from their quarry.

That was the way the White Eyes planned it.

That was not the way it would be.

Delcha straightened so suddenly that he banged his head against the low roof of the lookout. Ignoring the pain, he ducked outside. He bounded down the slope shouting for the band to mount up.

For once the White Eyes had underestimated him. He would ignore the quail until he had caught its young. Then, as he had planned it from the first, the quail would have to come to him.

Halfway down the slope the light picked him up, mockingly pointing the way for him as he ran. Without breaking stride, he raised his rifle in a silent gesture of defiance.

A fierce exultation lifted him up until he felt that he was an eagle soaring high above the earth, seeking out its prey.

Leaving the bodies of Bestinez and Seca inside the cave, he led the band straight north, away from the flashing light.

A thousand yards out, Donovan stuffed the mirror into his pocket and ran for his horse. The wily Apache had refused to take the bait. He was going after Tommy Lord instead.

Donovan wheeled the gray northward at the gallop. He had half a mile lead and he knew roughly where he was going; but it was not much of an advantage. His one chance of reaching the boy first lay in the distance he could put between himself and the Apaches – and then in how well he was able to use the time that distance gained him.

He gave the gray its head and felt its stride lengthen smoothly, effortlessly.

Run, you big, beautiful bastard! Run until you break that great heart of yours and then, by God, keep on running! That's what you were bred for!

By the time the Apaches had piled down the eight-hundred-foot 'mountain', Donovan had picked up another mile. Not much, but it would help.

A dozen miles further on, he cut Tommy Lord's trail in a small, oak brush clearing.

He knew it was Tommy because the pony's unshod hoofs had cut only shallow marks in the wet ground.

The boy was traveling slowly, either because he was hurt or the pony had gone lame. He had reined up here, not dismounting, for several minutes. The pony had been restless, churning up the ground in the area.

Studying the tracks, Donovan frowned.

Until he reached the clearing, Tommy Lord had been heading straight for the ranch. Now, inexplicably, he had turned due west and, traveling fast, put the pony toward the wild Sierra Anchas.

He had not been lost or confused. His course toward the ranch had been compass straight. His trail west was also straight. He had known exactly where he was and where he was going.

Mounting up, Donovan sat in his saddle a moment, thinking. Something had happened here in this clearing to make Tommy Lord deliberately turn away from safety and head for what he must have known was certain death.

You damned fool! Donovan thought. *You're just like your mother! All heart and no brains!*

He drove home the spurs and felt the big gray explode in a great surging leap. He made no effort to cover his trail as the racer ripped through the heavy oak brush. Speed was vital.

Two lives were at stake now, his and Tommy Lord's. The boy had served his purpose by drawing him into the open. If he were captured they would kill him on the spot.

Young Lord knew it, too. He had known it there in the clearing when he had deliberately chosen to draw the Apaches away from his mother and Pete.

It agonized Donovan to think that the boy may even have thought of him as well.

The gray was running effortlessly, although the rough terrain and heavy oak brush were bound to be taking their toll.

Twice, Donovan dismounted to study signs. The first time he estimated the tracks to be four, five hours old. The second time, his heart quickened. Tommy Lord had put his horse to the gallop. He must have realized that Delcha had cut his trail.

Once more Donovan sent the gray brush-popping down the slope. It was now well past mid-morning. Since dawn he had covered fifty miles, including thirty to Tonto Creek and back. Traveling west since the previous evening, Tommy Lord had put about that distance between himself and the ranch.

With real pursuit starting at the point where he had changed directions, the boy still held a good three or four hour lead. Just about this time, he should be entering the Sierra Anchas foothills. Once he got into the twisting, torturous maze of mountains, canyons and ravines, even Apaches would have trouble finding him.

Donovan touched the stallion's flanks with the spurs. The gray had begun to sweat lightly now, but showed no signs of faltering.

The country began to open up now, taking on the appearance of true desert. *Cholla*, barrel cactus, *ocotillo*, Spanish dagger, Joshua trees, an occasional *saguaro*, and sagebrush.

Roaring from northwest to southeast, the storm had missed his area. Heat, replacing the chill of the Rim country, plastered Donovan's shirt to his back and sapped the moisture from his body. At the first tiny creek, he dismounted and let the gray drink while he filled his canteen.

From the top of a small rock outcropping, he swept the country behind him with the field glasses. Seven or eight miles back a boiling cloud of dust was sweeping rapidly toward him. Further yet, but paralleling the cloud, two tiny specks were also closing in.

Donovan focused on the two riders. In a land where objects were greatly magnified, he could have spotted them with the naked eye. After a moment, he lowered the glasses with an explosive, 'Damn!'

They were riding straight to their deaths. If they were spotted Delcha would send two or three bucks back to finish them off. In open country, it would be quick and savage.

He had half expected Simpson to follow him. It was in keeping with the man's nature.

But Peggy! He had thought he would never see her again. Yet here she was, like a desperate extension of himself, following! Her presence complicated things. If they were attacked, he would be faced with the difficult decision of whether to ride back and help them, or to continue the race to save Tommy Lord.

Simpson should have ordered her to stay at the ranch where she would have been reasonably safe. Then he remembered Pete had no control over her.

Wilful, headstrong wench! What could you expect of young Lord? Like mother, like son!

Scrambling down the slope, he swung up

249

and headed west. The Simpsons would have to take care of themselves.

Around three o'clock, he rode into the foothills of the Sierra Anchas.

Shortly afterwards, he came upon the pony at the bottom of an arroyo, its neck broken.

A dozen feet away, Tommy Lord lay face down and naked in the scant shade of a Joshua tree.

Blistered, his body torn by brush and *cholla,* his wrists and ankles chafed by rawhide, and lips cracked by heat, it seemed impossible that he could have survived all that punishment.

Yet he had not only survived, he had done so despite two previous days of constant hunger, thirst, torture and storm exposure.

You've grown up overnight, boy, Donovan thought, forcing a trickle of water down the swollen throat. *You're a man now in a man's world. I'd hate to lose you.*

Tommy Lord stirred, half-strangled, but did not regain consciousness. His face was flushed, his breathing labored, his skin hot. Checking his pulse Donovan found it strong and irregular. There was an egg-shaped lump above his right temple where he had struck his head against a rock.

Squatted on his haunches, Donovan

studied the boy thoughtfully while he tried to rearrange his plans.

He knew the Sierra Anchas was well, if not better, then any man. If young Lord had been conscious and able to travel, there were half a dozen places where they could have forted up and make a fight of it. But it was useless to think about it now. The boy was in bad shape.

He would have to make a stand here.

Standing up, he scanned the thirty-foot wide arroyo with a professional eye. Water, none. No matter. The fight wouldn't last long enough for water to become a major problem. Shelter: the arroyo itself formed an excellent fortification. From its rim he would have a view of open country for a thousand yards.

Walking over to the gray, he untied his bedroll and with blanket, poncho and dead *ocotillo* branches erected crude lean-to over the boy.

Then, unsaddling the stallion, he climbed to the top of the arroyo. Crouched there, with only his head and shoulders visible, he scanned the country to the south and east with the field glasses.

His mouth tightened.

Time had run out.

From five hundred yards out he watched them come in, their horses sweat-lathered and throwing foam from the bits. Fanned out, with Delcha fifty yards in the lead, they raced across the cactus-studded land with reckless speed.

He counted them. *Seven*. He had been right.

Levering a shell into the Winchester, he waited.

Four hundred yards ... three hundred ... two hundred and fifty...

He drew a bead on Delcha. Outlined against the sky, the big Apache presented a perfect target.

Two hundred yards...

Donovan tightened up on the trigger.

A hundred and fifty...

No one could miss at that range.

Still Donovan hesitated.

By white men's standards, Delcha was a cruel, inhuman savage. But to Donovan, whose every waking moment for three weeks had been a battle of wits, courage and physical stamina with him, Delcha was something else.

He was an Apache chief, a man fighting a desperate, losing battle against a hated enemy who threatened everything he loved.

His freedom, his gods, the old ways...

If he fought that battle in the manner of his ancestors, ruthlessly and without mercy, it was for him the right way, the only way. Did not the White Eyes intend to steal his lands and exterminate him? Did not the Great Father's people offer a bounty for Apache scalps?

The Apache did not scalp.

He was wild, fierce, perhaps he was cruel. But in his own way was the White Eyes any less so?

Had he been an Apache, Donovan thought, he would have fought the same way and have also believed it right.

One hundred yards...

He swung the Winchester and killed the man on Delcha's left, then as quickly the one on his right.

At fifty yards, he dropped Delcha's horse. He could just as easily have killed the Apache. For the second time he had deliberately spared the Apache.

Delcha knew it.

As his horse went down, he leg-scissored off and turning, waved off the pack. Reining up, they sat their ponies in sullen silence while he walked forward.

Ten feet away, Delcha stopped.

Rifle ready, Donovan climbed out of the arroyo.

Warily, they sized up one another, not speaking.

For an Apache Delcha was a giant, and even bigger than Donovan. Only the legendary *Magnus Colorado*, who stood between six feet five and six feet seven inches tall, could have looked down upon him.

Yet it was his face that held Donovan's attention. Never had he seen a face so boldly reveal a man as did the Apache's. Fine featured, almost esthetic, with intense black eyes, an iron jaw, a wide, firm mouth, it was a chieftain's face. Arrogant, confident, crafty, merciless.

Like *Magnus Colorado*, he too had suffered much at the hands of the White Eyes. Now he killed and tortured in savage retaliation against those whose faces and crimes he had long since forgotten.

Only the bright, burning hate remained.

In that moment, Donovan was reminded of the day when, in the presence of Constance Farrington, Charles' hatred had also seared him.

Whatever Delcha may have thought of him as an adversary remained hidden behind the copper mask.

Pointing to Donovan's rifle, the Apache extended his hands, palms up, in a mocking gesture.

He had lost his rifle when his pony went down.

Without taking his eyes off Donovan, he drew the knife at his hip. Gently, he ran his thumb along the razor sharp edge.

Then he threw back his head and laughed.

Donovan accepted the challenge.

It was not quite the way he had planned it. He had wanted to drive a bargain with the Apache first. A promise to let the Simpsons and Tommy Lord go unharmed, win, lose, or draw. But after having seen the man, he realized now that it would be a waste of time. Whatever Delcha did would be of his own choosing.

The Simpsons and Tommy Lord were doomed.

If Delcha killed him, they would all die. If he killed Delcha, the pack would do the job.

He could of course shoot down the defenceless chief and perhaps two or three others before they killed him. There was even a fair chance that the survivors might flee back to the *rancheria* without bothering the Simpsons.

A snap shot from the hip would do.

Suddenly, he knew why Delcha had laughed. The Apache had not lost his rifle when his pony went down. He had deliberately thrown it away, knowing that the White Eyes would not shoot him.

Aiieee! He understood this man who, had he been an Apache, would have been his brother!

Now it would be a personal thing, settled between them with the knives.

Too late Donovan realized that he had been outwitted.

He dropped the Winchester and drew his own knife. He did not fear trickery. For Delcha was driven by some inner compulsion to kill his enemy fairly in hand to hand combat. He was at heart with 'feather' Indian.

As Delcha moved in, Donovan dropped into a crouch, knife arm half extended, and waited.

Three hundred yards away, Pete Simpson knelt behind a big boulder, watching through a pair of field glasses.

Hidden by the fast-traveling Apaches' dust, he and Peggy had stuck close behind the band throughout the long, hot day. Although they spoke but little, a common danger, a common purpose had drawn them into a kind of intimate truce.

In this less hostile atmosphere, Peggy Simpson relaxed. Once, pausing to rest the horses, she had almost told Pete of what had happened to her inside, and of this new, wonderful feeling she felt for him. But a sudden shyness set her to stammering like a school girl. And her confusion was compounded when Pete had regarded her with a quizzical smile. She had turned away, her face burning, and quickly mounted up.

It had been an experience which had both frightened and excited her.

But she was not thinking about that now. Her mind was on Donovan and her son.

As Simpson shifted the glasses, she asked quietly, 'Do you see Tommy?'

Simpson shook his head. 'No, but Donovan may have hidden him somewhere.'

'What's happening?'

Silently, he handed her the glasses.

When she returned them, her face was very pale. 'He doesn't have a chance, does he?'

'No,' Simpson said honestly. 'But they'll remember him.'

'Why did he throw away the rifle?' She turned an anguished face to her husband. 'Why didn't he shoot it out with them instead of... *Oh, damn!*' She buried her face in her hands.

'It's a personal thing with him,' Simpson told her. 'All mixed up with pride, principle, and wits. And, I guess you could say, raw courage. He's a special breed.'

She dropped her hands and scrambled to her feet. 'We've got to try and help him.'

Simpson jumped up and grabbed her around the waist. 'You want to get yourself killed!' He pulled her rifle from the boot and handed it to her. 'You stay here.'

From his own saddle bags he scooped up a handful of shotgun shells and stuffed them in his pockets. Then, carrying the Greener, he took off through the cactus and low brush.

'Pete, wait!' She ran after him, tripping over her long riding skirt and crying in angry frustration.

If they were all going to die, she didn't want it to happen without him knowing the truth.

Sand whisper of moccasins ... crunch of boots ... mounted riders with dark, sullen faces ... blaze of sunlight off shining steel.

Suddenly Delcha leaped in, his blade flicking across Donovan's belly, drawing blood and slicing dangerously deep. It was a smooth, well-executed move which Donovan only partially parried at the last instant.

A great joy filled Delcha's heart. Here was no clumsy fool to be stuck like a sheep herder. In the White Eye's hand the knife was an old friend.

To kill him in hand to hand combat – *Aiieee!* Throughout the *rancherias* the name of *Del-she* would be spoken of in the same breath with *Magnus Colorado,* Victorio, Cochise, Geronimo and Nachez.

He laughed aloud in sheer joy and, understanding, Donovan smiled.

After that, was a battle of wits.

They fought in the tradition of the classic knife fighter, an art virtually unknown outside of Spain save among the professional assassins retained by the *hidalgos* of Mexico, slim, cold-faced men whose trademarks were their leather clothing and the tiny, twin knives dangling at their wrists. As some men were artists with the violin, the paintbrush, or the pen, so were these assassins artists with the shining blades.

Rafael Medina, personal bodyguard to Maximo Baez y Baez, one of the most powerful *hidalgos* in Sonora, had taught Donovan the art in '78.

A captive assassin had been *Del-she's*

instructor years before. The Spaniard's reward had been the point of one of his own knives through his heart.

Apache and White Eyes had learned well.

As old men, those watching now would tell their grandsons of this fight to the death between an Apache war chief and a White Eyes worthy to have been one.

Circling, stomping their feet in the dust and waving their free hands to try and distract one another, they thrust, feinted, parried, attacked and counter-attacked, their blades weaving glittering patterns of light.

It was a thing to watch with wide eyes and long-held breath, feeling the hair at the nape of the neck rise at such skill, such courage – *aiieee!* – as the blood flowed freely down the sweating bodies.

Time and again, either fighter could have ended it with a handful of dust in the eyes, a kick in the groin, or a blow to the face with the free hand. But some deep sense of pride, some egotistical determination to prove himself the true master of the flickering blade held them in check.

Aiieee!

It was beautiful to watch and sad, too, because they were proud men, brave, merciless, men who could not live in the same world with one another.

Evenly matched as they were, it took a ruse on the part of one and a mistake on the part of the other to end it.

Retreating before a furious attack, Donovan suddenly stopped, turned sideways, and drew Delcha past him as a matador 'passes' a bull.

His knife passed cleanly between the ribs and into the Apache's heart.

Delcha died standing, his fierce black eyes hating his enemy to the last.

Wearily, Donovan turned away. He experienced no sense of personal triumph as he had thought he would. A brave man had died rather than see the old ways pass and a part of the Apache heritage had died with him. In a few years, the wild, fierce ones like *Del-she* and Victorio would be killed in battle and the remainder herded upon reservations to die of the white man's diseases or from inhospitable climates.

Delcha had known that and, like Chaco, had chosen to die a war chief.

Now, Donovan thought, it was his time to die.

Massive, uncompromising, he walked toward the silent Apaches. Blood spattered the dust with every step. He picked up his rifle, surprised that they did not kill him then.

A brave slipped from his pony and walked toward him leading a spare horse.

Another followed.

Donovan thumb-cocked his rifle.

The two Apaches tied Delcha on his pony and then mounted their own horses.

Silently, they reined away.

Watching them go, Donovan understood. Just as Delcha had known why he had been spared during the charge. Why the White Eyes had thrown away the rifle to fight hand to hand in a desperate gamble to save the boy and the woman. Bravery, even in a hated enemy, the Apache admired. Therefore he had ordered the White Eyes spared if he himself fell.

'He was a war chief, a brave man,' Donovan called after the band in Spanish. 'Take him back to the *rancheria* so that his people can mourn him.'

Wearily, he walked back to the arroyo. He was no longer a man with a purpose. The will that had kept him going for the past three weeks was gone. He felt empty, drained, conscious only of his many wounds: the bullet-gouged leg, the pain of his arms and slashed belly, the deep thrust just under his collar bone.

He half-slid, half tumbled to the bottom of the arroyo.

Under the blanket lean-to, Tommy Lord had not moved. But his breathing had eased, his pulse beat was almost normal, and his color was definitely better. Shade and water had helped.

Donovan forced a little water down his throat.

The boy sputtered, licked his lips and opened his eyes.

'You sure took your time!' he said weakly, and lapsed into an exhausted sleep.

Relief bowed Donovan's head.

He had not moved when the Simpsons scrambled to the bottom of the arroyo.

With a little cry, Peggy Simpson dropped down beside her son. 'Is he all right? He's not...?'

'He's got a lump on his head,' Donovan reassured her. 'And maybe a touch of sunstroke. But mostly he's just worn out from all he's been through.'

As she turned toward him, Peggy's eyes widened. 'My God! Pete, bring me a canteen, a blanket, and those bandages in my saddle bags!'

'It's not that bad,' Donovan protested, but

it was and he knew it. He was losing a lot of blood.

'Take off your shirt!'

Silently, he obeyed.

'Good God, he almost killed you!' Peggy Simpson exclaimed. 'A little deeper and you'd have spilled your whole insides!'

Staring down at the gaping, eight-inch slash, Donovan agreed that it wouldn't take much to tear the wound wide open.

'Are you in much pain?'

'Some.'

'I wish we had some whiskey.'

'I'll make out.'

When Simpson returned, Peggy washed out the wounds and bound them with clean strips from an old petticoat she had brought along just in case. A long foot-wide strip of the blanket she wound tightly around Donovan's waist like a sash. It let him breathe, but that was about all.

'That ought to hold you in if you ride slowly.'

She turned a worried face to her husband. 'Pete, we've got to get him to a doctor.'

'There's a little town ten miles southwest of here,' Simpson said. 'I think there's a doctor there. Why don't you ride in with Donovan and I'll bring Tommy in after sundown.'

Squinting up at the sun, Donovan said, 'It should be cool enough to travel with the boy in another hour. We'll wait. Meanwhile, let's get him out of this arroyo. It's like an oven.'

He tried to rise, couldn't make it. He lifted a gray, perspiring face to the rancher.

'Give me a hand, will you?'

Simpson helped him to his feet. 'You think you can make it?'

'I'll make it.'

Painfully, he worked his way to the top of the arroyo with Simpson carrying Tommy Lord and Peggy leading the horses.

A faint breeze cooled their faces as they reached level ground. A hundred yards out they found a small island of shade in the lee of a huge boulder.

Wearily, they stretched out on the still-warm sand.

Peggy splashed a little water over Tommy's face. He mumbled a protest but did not awaken. She turned an anxious face toward Donovan.

'Are you sure he's all right?'

Donovan nodded. 'He's been through a lot. He'll probably sleep like that for twenty-four hours.'

Kneeling there, she studied Donovan with grave, troubled eyes.

'Why did you throw away the rifle?' she asked. 'Did Delcha promise to spare Tommy if you fought him hand-to-hand?'

'No.'

'But you were gambling that he would?'

'Yes.'

Stretching out beside him, she propped herself on her elbows, her long, black hair brushing his face.

'You could have died horribly, you know.'

Donovan said nothing.

'Why did you do it?' she persisted. 'Why didn't you ride back to Tucson when you had the chance? What makes you the kind of man you are anyway?'

'Does a man have to have a reason for everything he does?' Donovan retorted. 'Isn't it enough that he does it? Why did your son deliberately risk his life to try and draw Delcha away from the ranch? He did, you know. But don't ask him why. Just be proud that he did it.'

'You mean that he ... for me ... after what he knows?' Peggy Simpson gave an anguished little cry. *'Oh, my God!'*

'And just what does he know?' Donovan asked gently. 'Except that mothers are human, too. I suspect that he's already for-given you. In time, he'll forget completely.'

The brilliant blue eyes switched to Pete Simpson. 'Some people never forgive – or forget.'

Simpson regarded her steadily. In the late afternoon sun his face remained expressionless. 'People think too much about forgiving and forgetting instead of changing,' he said. 'When the one happens it usually takes care of the others.'

Had he waited a moment longer, or had she spoken an instant sooner, it would have all been resolved. But while she hesitated, Simpson turned abruptly away and the chance was lost.

After that they lapsed into silence, isolated from one another by the past yet closer in understanding than ever before.

At dusk the three of them mounted up and with Simpson carrying the boy rode slowly toward town.

The week spent in Pine while Donovan and Tommy Lord recovered began also to heal the deeper wounds of the spirit.

It had been a shattering experience for all of them. Yet from it each emerged with a keener insight into his own nature, as well as an appreciation of one another.

For Peggy Simpson it was a resolution of

purpose, a realization of what she wanted from life.

From the day they rode into Pine with Donovan holding to his saddle horn and Pete carrying Tommy, she put up a wall between herself and Donovan.

Out there in the meadow that morning of the chase she had made her decision.

She would not let her feelings for Donovan destroy her marriage.

The river of fire within her was dead, along with the hate which had driven her to use her body in a vain effort to strike back at a sanctimonious father.

Her newly discovered love for her husband was both comforting and down to earth. Her son had begun to accept Pete as a father. And Pete, beneath his frustration, had always loved the boy.

Whether he would ever love her again was another matter. To a large extent it would depend upon what she was able to do with her own life. She was thirty-two years old. She had nothing to show for those years save sordid memories. Nor was there any assurance that she could do any better in the future.

She did have several things working strongly in her favor. She had given up her hate for her father. She had conquered the fire in her body. She had given up the doll. And now she was giving up Donovan.

In essence, she was removing every obstacle that stood in the way of what she wanted most out of life.

Pete, her son, her home.

She had always felt it was she who needed people, never that others might need her. Tommy, as any boy, needed his mother. Pete needed her because, for him, the fullness of life could be attained only by sharing it with a woman. He had gotten a sorry bargain when he had married her. Given time perhaps she could change that – and herself in the process.

Only Donovan threatened her future.

Donovan – and herself.

For already those few hours they had shared in the mow – his understanding, tolerance and amazing gentleness, everything that had helped her to a final understanding of herself – were woven into the warp and woof of her spirit. Even the thought of them being torn from her was intolerable.

Yet she knew that she must do it.

There could never be any future for her and Donovan. The thing between them was simply too big to live with. Eventually it would engulf her, leaving her with no identity save as a reflected image of him. She would cling to him as she had clung to the doll, living in a world of dreams, never becoming the woman she was capable of being.

The price was too high.

That knowledge helped strengthen her resolve.

Thereafter, she never visited Donovan unless Pete was with her. Yet each time she saw him was a hurt, a sham. She wanted to lie beside him, her head on his shoulder and, feeling warm and secure, tell him why she was treating him this way.

But he already understood, just as he had understood about the doll. He had led her to solid ground, given her confidence, and then forced her to look within herself for her answers.

She knew what she owed him. She knew also that he would not want her to pay it.

He had already given her her life. Now he was giving her a chance to save her marriage.

Perhaps it was too late. At best, it would not be an easy road. She realized that in the future Pete would dominate their marriage. She did not mind. She had always wanted him to be the head of the family. But he would have to understand that she would walk beside him, not behind him. She would share the responsibility. They would talk over their problems. Then she would let him think that it was he who made the final decision.

Yes, she would make him a good wife. And she would grow and mature as a woman because she would always know that he and Tommy needed her.

Whenever she visited Donovan she always kept this in mind. It gave her the strength to keep up the cool, impersonal front.

But it never stilled the hammering of her heart.

Donovan's reaction to the situation was to quietly withdraw into himself. He remained as courteous and thoughtful as ever. He simply did not put the Simpsons in the position of having to make lame excuses for their brief visits.

He understood why they stayed away. His presence was a painful reminder to Pete Simpson of what had happened up there in the mow. And Peggy was still afraid of her emotions.

Perhaps it was better this way. He had already brought them enough trouble. With it clear that they were moving closer together than at any time since their marriage, he had no desire to upset things.

Nevertheless he found the abrupt separation difficult. Peggy Simpson had aroused within him a need, an all but forgotten hunger for a woman's love.

While he was recovering he did a great deal of thinking about her, about himself, and about the two of them.

He sensed that she had decided to stay with her husband and that Simpson was willing to try and make a go of things. With Tommy Lord's acceptance of his stepfather they were now a family united.

Yet the bond between himself and Peggy Simpson remained as strong as ever. She knew it, he knew it, and Simpson knew it. She betrayed herself every time she looked at him, spoke to him, or even entered the room.

She had rejected him with her mind, but not with her heart.

It was not a happy thought. For Donovan knew there could never be any future for the two of them together. They came from different worlds. Their backgrounds, their values, even their philosophies were different. Whatever this thing was between them, it could never survive the pressures of everyday living.

For two days, they had lived out of time in an isolated world of violent passions – loving, fighting, hating, sharing – their true natures emerging as the tensions mounted.

During that period they had come to know one another as few people ever did. They no longer labored under any illusions as to who they were, what they were, or why they were. *They knew.*

They had also found in one another something that was not really there – a nobility of spirit that sometimes, in war or in situations of great stress, lifts an individual above and beyond what they are. Once, but seldom twice.

Peggy Simpson still clung to that single fact. Disillusion later could destroy her. *Cherish the idea, but avoid the reality.* There could be no harm in that. In time, she and her husband would grow to know, understand and accept one another. Already they had found themselves and what they wanted from life.

Donovan was still searching, but that search, although he did not yet realize it, was no longer related to Peggy Simpson.

They stood quietly in front of the stage line

office, not talking because that which was between them could not be expressed in words.

Already Donovan had the strange feeling that they were moving slowly, inexorably apart. Not because they wished it so, but because some inner instinct told them that their futures lay in opposite directions.

Beside him, Peggy Simpson must have sensed his thoughts for suddenly she turned toward him, her eyes meeting his with a startled expression.

She caught her breath. It was as though she were back on the ranch, staring down at him asleep under the big oak with the sun dappling his face and her feeling that if he opened his eyes he would know her for what she was, what she had been and what she was becoming. And that unless he left immediately she would have no secrets from him and no escape.

She must have been gifted with second sight.

From the beginning, she had never had any secrets from him. He had always known her. At any time, he could have destroyed her. He still could. For he had only to ask her and she would go with him, forgetting Pete, Tommy, all of her firm resolutions. Knowing it couldn't last yet not caring so long as she could hold on to the moment.

With him she had found something, a beauty, an inner peace of mind which she knew she would never again find with another human being. To give it up now, to let it slip through her fingers...

Panic-stricken, she turned a white face toward her husband, who stood watching her without expression. 'Please, Pete...'

Silently, Simpson motioned to Tommy Lord and walked away.

The boy hesitated, looking at Donovan with grave eyes. His young face no longer bore the smug arrogance of ten days ago.

'I don't reckon God will ever make another one like you,' he said. 'Leastways I sure hope not. Two of you could sure turn the world upside down. Just the same, if I could have my druthers I'd druther be like you than any man living, except maybe you an' Pete together.'

His face took on a strained expression. 'I ain't going to say good-bye 'cause I figure you'll sort of always be around one way or the other. I'm just going to walk away like I was ... like I was...' He wheeled and ran toward the waiting stage.

'He'll grow up trying to be like you,' Peggy Simpson said. 'I hope he can. Then I'll never lose you completely.'

With a little sigh, she moved against him and laid her head upon his chest. For a moment, she remained thus, feeling warm and secure, like she had up there in the hay mow a thousand years ago.

Then in a low, calm voice, she said, 'I don't think I can go through with it. I don't think I can get in that coach and ride away as though you didn't exist.' She lifted an anguished face to him, trying to understand this thing that had happened to her.

'How can you fear and hate and love someone all at the same time?' she asked. 'And then end up having them become a part of you. *How?*'

'Love and hate and fear are mixed up in everyone,' Donovan said. 'Maybe it's because men and women are natural enemies but can't do without one another. I don't know.'

'I'm a romantic fool, aren't I?'

'No.'

She became so still that he thought she must be holding her breath. 'If it weren't for Pete would you take me with you?'

'Would you want to go?'

'Yes.' Raising her head, she smiled up at him through her tears. 'But it wouldn't have worked, would it?'

'I don't know.'

'But you would have taken me with you?'

'Yes.'

'As your wife.'

'No other way.'

Her mouth quivered. 'You make me feel both proud and humble. I'll always remember that.'

A small man with sunburned features stepped out of the stage line office, checked his watch, and nodded pleasantly to them.

'Best get aboard, Ma'am,' he said. 'We'll be pulling out in a couple of minutes.'

'Thank you.'

The stage driver tipped his hat and walked away.

She laid her head back on Donovan's chest, pretending she was back in the mow, lying in his arms in the sweet-smelling hay, drifting off to sleep. She closed her eyes and listened to the swift flowing creek, her emotions all mixed up with this man beside her.

'Donovan...' the sound of the rushing water was growing fainter, 'you are a fantastic man.'

'And you are a fantastic woman.'

'Donovan, I...'

'All aboard, Ma'am!'

She raised her head. Her face was rice-powder white.

'Oh, Donovan, what am I going to do without you!'

'Pete's a good man, Peggy. And then there's your son. They both need you.'

'I know that,' she cried. 'But it's not the same!'

He nodded toward the stagecoach where Simpson and Tommy Lord stood waiting patiently. 'You know why you loved the doll, Peggy? Not because it loved you but because it *needed* you. That's what you've craved all your life. To be needed. Well, they need you.'

She brushed futilely at her tears. 'You don't need anyone! You've never needed anyone!'

An odd expression softened Donovan's face. 'I needed you.'

'But now you're sending me away!'

'Because I want you to be happy.'

'How can I be happy knowing I'll never see you again?'

Something flickered in Donovan's eyes. 'No matter where I am,' he said, 'I'll never be very far away from you. Remember that.'

A peace came over Peggy Simpson. Now she could do what she had not had the courage to do before.

Standing on tip-toes, she kissed him, letting all her love pass to him through her lips. Then drawing away, she smiled up at him and in a voice that broke a little, said, 'Good-bye, Donovan.'

It was the longest walk she would ever make, those twenty steps to the waiting stage, but she made them, her head high and the tears rolling freely down her cheeks.

Beside the coach, she turned and, for the last time, looked at Donovan. Massive, virile, wonderfully human, his face, even in this moment, as calm as when she had first seen him lying asleep under the big oak.

That was the way she would remember him.

She caught her breath, then turned to her husband and said in a low voice, 'I'm ready, Pete.'

Silently Simpson helped her aboard.

The driver laid the popper of his nine-foot whip alongside the high leader's ears and shouted, 'Hi-ya! Hi-ya!'

The team broke into a smart trot, dust spinning from the stage's wheels as they picked up speed.

Seated between her husband and her son, Peggy Simpson stared straight ahead, her hands folded in her lap, her eyes tear-dimmed. A part of her life was flowing away behind her like a swift rushing river and there was nothing she could do to stop it. Yet even as it was flowing away from her she felt herself moving upstream against the current into the future.

She had always thought of herself as a tiny chip being swept downstream to inevitable destruction. Suddenly it occurred to her that she had learned how to swim against the current to the *Source*.

'Don't cry, Ma!' Tommy pleaded. 'Please don't cry!'

With a quiet smile, she drew him to her and said in a serene voice, 'Women always cry when they say good-bye to someone special, Tommy. It's their nature. But then they get over it.'

She turned to Pete, her eyes candid, asking. 'All they need is a little time.'

Pete laid his hand over hers in a mute gesture of understanding.

The town lay behind them now and the team had settled down to a smooth, steady pace.

She laid her head back against the seat, closed her eyes, and let her mind float free.

'You're a fantastic man, Donovan!'

'And you're a fantastic woman.'

'That's what you've craved all your life. To be needed.'

'How can I be happy when I'll never see you again!'

'No matter where I am I'll never be very far away from you.'

She fell asleep with the memory of clean, fresh smelling hay beneath her and the swift rushing waters of the creek in her ears and her hand resting trustfully in her husband's.

Standing in the street, Donovan watched until the stage disappeared into the distance. Then he walked slowly toward the hotel.

Two doors away, he turned into the *Crystal Palace*. Ordering bourbon, he stood alone at the bar, studying his reflection in the long mirror.

She was gone, even at this moment moving steadily farther and farther away from him. He tried not to think of it, his mind clinging to that last moment when she had raised herself on tip-toes and given him her lips.

But somehow the memory became subtly intertwined with a series of kaleidoscopic thoughts that kept changing so fast that they all ran together.

...*Long black hair, startling blue eyes, soft,*

pliant body, and then she was running toward the cabin

...Outlined against the sky in glorious, free flight

...Owing you my life, Mister Donovan, doesn't mean I have to like you

...Well, don't just stand there gawking like a clod! Help me dismount!

...If you don't leave this place tonight, I'm going to kill you!

...You're a strange boy! I don't think I've ever met anyone like you before!

...I'm not going to risk my life for the sake of a damned bounty hunter!

...I'll bet you've never even kissed a girl, have you?

...Damn you, Donovan, for a... Ah, Donovan!...

...I ... never ... found ...her! Not even one of her little shoe-button eyes!...

...Oh, Donovan! Now I've ruined everything! He'll never let me see you again! I know by the way he acted...

...How can I be happy knowing I'll never see you again!...

...Remember me! Remember me!...

...Oh, Donovan, what am I going to do without you?...

...I'll never forget you, Donovan!...

...I don't think I can do it. I don't think I can ride away from here as though you never existed...

...Remember, I was the first!

...Good-bye, Donovan.

...Remember! Remember!

He put down his glass and walked out.

An hour later, he rode southward astride the gray stallion he had bought from Pete Simpson for five hundred dollars.

A sense of urgency drove him now. There were many matters to be taken care of. He had to see Carmela Ortega, arrange to send Victorio to Spain, set up a trust fund for Tommy Lord's education, and secretly guarantee any bank loan Pete Simpson might ever need.

After that, he would have to think.

Perhaps what he was seeking was beyond his reach. Perhaps for him it had always been unattainable. He would have to find out for himself. But not until he had separated the black and gold threads so tightly woven into the fabric of his life.

Only then would he know.

Reining up, he turned in his saddle and looked toward the Mogollons stretching across the distant horizon. For a long time he sat motionless, his hands resting on the saddle horn, feeling the warmth of Peggy Simpson's mouth on his.

She was a part of him; she would always be a part of him. But – and there was a sadness in the thought – as the distance between past and future widened so also would the bond between them weaken until at last they were free of everything save the memory.

Wheeling the gray, he headed south.

He had a long way to go.

A long, long way.

The publishers hope that this book has given you enjoyable reading. Large Print Books are especially designed to be as easy to see and hold as possible. If you wish a complete list of our books please ask at your local library or write directly to:

The Golden West Large Print Books
Magna House, Long Preston,
Skipton, North Yorkshire.
BD23 4ND